SECRETS OF THE DHAMPIR

RENEE JOINER

OSHUN
PUBLICATIONS
oshunpublications.com

RENEE JOINER

SECRETS
OF THE
DHAMPIR

Secrets of the Dhampir by Renee Joiner
Published by Oshun Publications
9 Old Kings Road STE. 123 #1038
Palm Coast, FL 32137
www.oshunpublications.com

Book Design by Miblart
miblart.com

ISBN 978-1-961362-09-3 (Paperback)
ISBN 978-1-961362-10-9 (Hardback)
ISBN 978-1-961362-08-6 (eBook)

SINGLE TITLES BY RENEE

The Monsters and the Morally Ambiguous

Tread carefully in a landscape where monsters walk among us, and morality is as fluid as the shapes they assume.

Tempest
Dead Wrong
Her Dark Pleasure

The Vengeful and the Vindicated

Venture into the shadowy realm of personal retribution, where the line between hunter and hunted becomes blurred.

Half Demon
Wanted Undead or Alive
Witch's Justice
Ancestor's Magic
Red Rising

The Supernatural Sleuths and Arcane Artifacts

Prepare to delve into a world where the supernatural is woven into the fabric of everyday life.

My Soul to Reap
Vance and Vance
Cold Read
That's the Spirit
Magic Huntress
Relic Huntress
While You Were Reaping

The Cursed and the Powerful

Dive into stories of latent legacies and untamed powers, where characters grapple with the dangerous gifts bestowed upon them.

Gravetide
Strange Magic
Blade of the Guild
Brewing Up a Storm

SERIES BY RENEE

Thorne Sisters Chronicles

Possessed by Magic
  Reincarnated by Magic
  Immortal by Magic

Magic of the Night

Raven Magic

CHAPTER 1
BLOODLUST

It's dead silent as Nietta Williams lies staring into the white abyss of her bedroom ceiling. All she can hear is the persistent *thump—thump—*thumping of her heart beating against her ear drums. Once again, she has woken up in the middle of the night to a familiar ache blooming inside the pits of her stomach. It begins as a warm sensation that spreads through her body and sends tingles through her nerves, rapidly turning into a searing heat that burns the entire surface of her skin. She can feel sweat start to prickle on the edges of her temples, becoming more unbearable the more she tries to force it down. Despite having opened all of her windows, her body's temperature refuses to decrease.

Her gaze shifts toward the outside, barely making out the shape of the full moon through her sheer curtains fluttering in the breeze. It isn't the first time that she is overcome by the aching lust for blood. Ever since her fangs grew in at the age of sixteen, she has found it near impossible to satiate her sporadic cravings. The desire fills up her entire mind and overrides every thought with its incessant urging to feed.

The hunger has become like a friendly devil that constantly sits on her shoulder whispering sweet nothings into her ear as she continuously attempts in vain to ignore its alluring temptations. In a last-ditch effort to silence her mind, Nietta reaches for her phone. The glaring light of her screen causes her to wince. She stares at the time, 2:13 a.m. *That's a whole two hours earlier than last time,* she thinks. She opens her phone and navigates to her unopened texts. There is one from Vanessa, one from her hair salon advertising their newest event, and then one from her mother.

It has been a while since she responded to or even opened one of her mother's messages. They hadn't spoken in months and when they did speak it never lasted any longer than a few minutes just to check in. Their relationship had been rocky at best since Nietta's vampire form first began to appear. A rift between the two arose after they found that they disagreed on an increasing number of decisions surrounding Nietta's life and how she wanted to live it.

Her finger moves to open the conversation when she is overcome by the sudden onslaught of aching pangs reminding her of her ravenous hunger. Her legs slide over the edge of her bed, the moon's reflection bouncing off her dark skin like a mark of the night reminding her of her shackles. It's a fate that she just can't seem to escape, suffering alone in her own paradox with the human part of her—the weaker half—battling a doomed fight to keep the vampire within at bay.

She rushes to the bathroom to splash cold water against her flesh, like a slap in the face against her heightened senses. Her body is quickly descending into its hunting mode and Nietta is losing control. Every muscle in her body is tensed up as she tries to stave off the hunger for just a second longer but the moment her eyes meet her own in the mirror, she can tell from her growing pupils that she can no longer wait.

Throwing on a hoodie and a pair of jeans, she makes for

the door. *Time to quench this bitch,* she thinks as she slips into the night.

———

Outside the Newport Blood Bank, Nietta stares up at the building looming over her. In the darkness, it looks more intimidating than it does during the day. It gives off a more sinister and chilling vibe. Somehow, even the building itself makes her feel unwelcome, reminding her that she really shouldn't be here.

She is flooded by conflicting emotions at her repulsion toward having to steal blood and the excitement of sinking her teeth into one of the plastic bags, finally ridding herself of her relentless hunger. Usually, she would have a stash of animal blood hidden away at home to satiate her thirst, but due to the influx of tourists recently, hunting hasn't been a safe choice as of late. As she hasn't had the chance to restock her supply, she is left with the one option that she wished to avoid.

There is no more time to waste. The cravings are growing at an alarming rate and if she waits any longer, she might just reach the point of losing all control.

Pulling her hood up, she ducks her head down and makes for the side of the building, careful to avoid being caught by the security cameras. Just as she is about to turn the corner to the rare exit, she is hit by the mumbling of voices. She stops in her tracks.

"Where's your money?" asks a gruff voice. From the tone and inflection, she can tell that it must be a man somewhere in his mid-twenties to thirties. He sounds agitated, almost as if he is uncomfortable with his aggression.

"It-it's in the dashboard," the second voice replies. This one sounds older, most likely in his early seventies. He's afraid.

The familiar pull inside her stomach returns, begging for her attention. She rolls her eyes back into her head as she lets out a frustrated sigh. *This isn't the time to get involved in other people's business,* she thinks trying to justify walking away. If she goes to play the hero in this situation, she might just end up losing control and hurting someone.

Deciding to see if she can wait them out, she squats down behind the corner of the building. Now observing them from the shadows, she watches as the mugger drags the old man around by his arm as he searches the passenger side of his car. He is rushed and very clearly a rookie. He's got one hand occupied with his victim and the other rummaging around while gripping onto a knife.

Despite the lack of streetlamps in the parking lot, Nietta can rely on her night vision and vampire abilities to make out the familiar balding, gray head and round figure of her neighbor, Mr. Salinger. They've greeted each other a few times, and he's always been kind to her, but Nietta knows that it is near impossible for her to provide him with any help.

Although hunched over, she can tell that the mugger stands at about 5 ft 10 inches, is dressed in all black, and is patently favoring his right leg over his left. He's thrown a few of his findings out onto the ground as he has no hands to carry the items. He's very obviously preparing to bag everything once he's done and make a run for it. All she can hope for is that he finds what he needs and takes off as soon as possible.

A few more seconds pass and Nietta can feel the predator inside of her growing more and more impatient. *Any second now.* But they don't part ways and even though it has only been a few minutes, she has finally reached a breaking point. *This won't do.*

She runs through the building layout in her head. Knowing the entrances and exits like the back of her hand from her endless history of visits helps her figure out a way in which she can slip into the building unnoticed. Just as she turns to head in the other direction, a loud thunk and a hissing sneer are heard from the assailant. Nietta feels the rush before she takes notice of the smell. Blood. He must have tripped over his own feet and sliced himself, that darned idiot.

She can't lose hold of her restraint, not here, not now. A few more curses continue to fly in the background as she tries to slow her breathing, but the reins of control are already slipping through her fingers. Her eyes have already dilated to the size of the full moon. A black void spreads out and she can feel her lips stretch into a lopsided grin.

Finally, a voice echoes inside her mind. *Time to party.*

Nietta lurches into a standing position and emerges from the shadows like a stealthy feline. Her eyes glow with ecstasy as she moves toward the two men who have now caught notice of her presence. They both freeze in their positions half off the ground. The assailant had tripped over his bad leg and managed to drag Mr. Salinger down with his steel-like grip. They are caught off guard by the addition of a third party to the scene and as she passes under a streetlamp recognition takes over Mr. Salinger's expression while the assailant noticeably tenses up.

"Nietta?" Mr. Salinger calls out as she approaches. "Is that you?"

But Nietta's human side has vanished and her vampire side is out to feed, not to play friendly neighbor. "Hi, boys." She grins as the assailant's eyes grow wide.

"Your teeth—" Before he can finish Nietta is already on top of him sinking her fangs into his neck. The sweet, sweet taste of blood fills her mouth. She loses herself in the euphoric sensation that takes over her body and eases all her suffering. The man struggles and screams, trying to break free from her grip but her strength overpowers him like a lioness would a fly.

If there is one thing that Nietta has come to understand over the years is that human blood, unlike animal blood, is like an aphrodisiac to vampires. Especially for dhampirs whose human half makes their self-resistance weaker than a full vampire's. Once control has been lost, it is hopeless to pull her out of her feeding trance until the very last drop has been consumed.

Mr. Salinger lies just beneath the two, staring at the scene unfolding before his eyes in shock. He jumbles his words and suddenly finds the power to crawl away, get in the car, and drive off before Nietta even gets the chance to consider him her next prey.

Although completely immersed in her feeding, Nietta takes notice of Mr. Salinger's exit but pays it no mind. She'll deal with it later.

A voice deep inside of her screams to be let out, to chase down Mr. Salinger and explain that it's all a mistake. To explain that she doesn't want it to be this way, she didn't want to hurt anyone. But, the human inside of her has locked away in the catacombs of her soul and won't come out until the deed is already done.

With a final breath of struggle and a single convulsion, the man falls limp in her arms. She lets go and drops her head back in satisfaction. Above her, she sees the stars and as the blood dribbles down the side of her chin, she realizes what she's done.

The human in her takes over and the man's body is dropped to the ground. "Oh, my god," she whisper-screams. "What have I done?"

She whips her head around, double-checking that she is indeed alone. Alone with a dead man. The man she killed.

Crouching at his side, her shaky hand reaches for the side of his throat and aimlessly searches for a pulse. A pulse that she already knows is gone. She must keep going. She must get rid of the body. She wraps the fabric of his black hoodie into her grip and chucks him over her back like she would if she were giving him a piggyback. Without thinking, Nietta takes off into the woods behind the parking lot. She feels the wind biting her cheeks as she runs at super speed. The branches swipe at her skin as she effortlessly makes her way through the overgrown brush and into the depths of the trees.

Had it been different if she'd just been able to hang on for a second longer? Could it have been different?

She doesn't stop until she is in another forest in the next town over. She finds a spot that she deems good enough and bends down to dig a hole with her bare hands like a dog. A hole that would have taken a human day to create.

Once finished, she stands over it, losing herself in the emptiness of its depth, contemplating what she could have done differently. Her eyes trace the scar on the man's left cheek, his lifeless brown eyes like two bullet holes in his head, and his icy lips now dull and drained of all color. Up close he looks so real, so human. Perhaps he was a bad man doing a bad thing but that didn't mean he deserved to die. At least not at the hands of a monster.

Nietta rolls him over onto the edge of the hole and lets him fall with a thunk. "I'm so sorry," she whispers as she fills the hole, letting her shock consume her thoughts like the earth consumes his body.

———

Fog paints the bathroom mirror like an early morning mist after a turbulent thunderstorm. Nietta reaches out with her towel to wipe off a section of the fog to see her reflection. She stares into her eyes trying to search for any trace of what happened last night. They stare back at her like empty pits. Somewhere in the darkness of her soul is a vampire, reposing in satisfaction at their successful hunt.

After having buried the body, Nietta had wasted no more

time in finding Mr. Salinger in his kitchen on the line with the police. He was describing a vicious monster to the operator, arguing with them that he knew what he saw and that he wasn't crazy. *He isn't crazy*, she thought to herself as she approached him from behind, *just a little too slow.*

"Mr. Salinger," Nietta said as she slid a hand onto his shoulder. He whipped around and instantly dropped the phone in shock. She could hear the woman on the line call out in confusion.

"You— you—" He fumbled for the words and attempted to scramble away from her grip on his shoulder.

"I know," she said, trying her best to sound as soothing as possible. Her eyes found his bright blue ones glazed in fear. She lured his subconscious into a trance-like state. "Mr. Salinger, you were out in the parking lot of the Newport Blood Bank tonight to have a little smoke and get away from your wife after an argument. You took some time to yourself and went home. You didn't see anyone there. It was an uneventful night." She held their eye contact as he repeated the words back to her. "You're gonna pick up the phone, and tell the lady that she is right, you just had a strange episode. Tell her you are feeling better now and sorry for wasting her time."

Nietta leans into the mirror satisfied with her ensemble, dressed in a black pencil skirt, black tights, and a white loose button-up with a beige overcoat thrown on top of the outfit. She brushes over her edges with her fingertips and the tight bun she has pulled her hair back into, double-checking they are secured in place. For the final touch, she whips out her matte burgundy lipstick.

Leaning into the mirror, she smudges the pigment across her lips and pulls back in satisfaction. One final glance before she takes off in the hopes that she can keep her mind as neat as her appearance for the rest of the day.

"Nietta," a familiar voice shrills as she steps into the office.

Coffee in one hand and clipboard in the other, Vanessa scrambles over to her side the second she gets off the elevator. "Where the *hell* have you been, girl?"

Nothing escapes the hawk-like eyes of Vanessa. She is the receptionist at their office and therefore retains all the gossip and loves to know every little detail about everyone's waking moment. Since Nietta is her best friend at the office, she has found that Vanessa has her cute little button nose even deeper in her business than anyone else's.

"I slept in." She shrugs, trying to make haste toward her cubicle, hoping that Vanessa is the only one that noticed her tardiness.

She halts in her tracks as Nietta places her purse on her desk and begins to unpack the necessary items for the day. A tumbler, her phone, and a breakfast bar.

"Don't give me that," Vanessa retorts, giving Nietta a deadpan look. "You are never late. That is just not like you at all." Her perfectly arched eyebrows twist in confusion as she gives her usual 'I'm-not-leaving-till-you-explain' pout.

Nietta looks at her friend's youthful, round face, and doe-like eyes that innocently beg to be let in. She tries to imagine what her reaction might be if she told her the truth. In her mind, an image of Vanessa staring at her with an expression of fear and disgust pops up, and she is quickly shaken back to reality.

"I've just been having a rough couple of nights," she responds. "I think my insomnia has just been wearing me out a bit."

Vanessa nods slowly seemingly letting it go. "Oh, well I can recommend you some vitamins." She taps at the clipboard in her right arm with her acrylic nails. Nietta feels herself hone in on the rhythmic tapping, finding that the noise is getting strangely louder.

"Oh, yeah." Nietta shakes her head trying to dismiss the weird feeling she is getting. "That would be helpful."

Vanessa straightens up and breaks out with a proud smile. "Great, I'll go grab them from my desk."

Vanessa's caramel brown curls whip through the air in slow motion as she turns to walk away. The *tap–tap–tapping* of her heels echoed against the wooden floor unusually.

Falling into her office chair, she pulls out the keyboard and opens up her desktop. *Time to focus*. Not a second after opening her email, she hears a weird thumping in the background increasing in volume at an alarming rate.

Her fingers hover over her keyboard as she looks around the office. Nothing seems out of the ordinary. None of her other colleagues seem to notice the sound, so she tries to brush it off and continue focusing. But the thumping continues and multiplies. Multiple rhythmic thumps are overlapping in the background and Nietta finally acknowledges that her senses are heightening.

Fuck, she thinks as she picks up on details that she otherwise can't see with her human vision. The dust particles lined the spaces between the keys on her keyboard, the tiny hair follicles in her skin. The heartbeats of her colleagues continue to thump away in the background like an orchestra picking up intensity.

Her breath fills up her thoughts as she squeezes her eyes shut, hoping to block out her environment. She just fed, but for some reason, the cravings have returned almost tenfold.

"Nietta?" a voice calls out in the distance. "You okay?"

She can feel Vanessa hovering over her desk and when she opens her eyes, she notices the bottle of vitamins that she rattles around in her hand.

"I got you the vitamins," Vanessa says, but Nietta is lost in the flurry of sensory overstimulation. Not only can she hear the vitamins bouncing around their container, but she can also feel them.

"I'm not feeling so good." She pushes away from her desk and shoves all of her things back into her purse. "I'm—" she attempts to explain to Vanessa that she is going home for the day when she hears the slice of a finger against a piece of paper and a muttered curse that follows. Blood.

She manages to dodge past Vanessa and bolts toward the elevator just as it opens. As she spirals mentally, Nietta finds herself unable to maneuver around the person stepping into the office, smacking straight into their right arm.

"Woah—" the voice pipes up, completely caught off guard.

Their eyes meet and for a second the world freezes. She feels a pull toward the manly gaze that pierces hers.

"Is this a circus or a workplace?" the man snaps at her. His warm blue eyes quickly turn into cold, hard stones and she mutters an apology before escaping into the elevator that was just about to close.

She lets out a shaky breath. She can hear somewhere in the distance, from the office she just escaped, Vanessa apologizing to the man for her. But she blocks them out and decides—tourist season or not, she needs to find a deer to sink her teeth into. Right now.

CHAPTER 2
RETURN OF THE PAST

The world rushes back in as Nietta slowly slips out of her deep sleep. For a second she forgets where she is until the shaking of her side table from the relentless vibrations of her phone drags her out of her stupor. She groans, rubbing her hands down her face.

The day before she had been sent into overdrive after feeding twice in two days. Blood rush if you will. After reaching a peak in heightened vampire senses and abilities, Nietta had completely crashed and lost track of time. For one reason or another, the last week has not been treating her very well.

She grabs at her phone and lets out a frustrated breath as she realizes she has to sit up to reach it.

Vanessa: Nietta, you okay?

Vanessa: Where are you?

Vanessa: Why aren't you answering?

Vanessa: The new CEO wants a team meeting at 9!

Vanessa has been bombarding her with texts ever since

she left the office in a hurry. The last one read twenty minutes ago.

"Oh no," she mutters as she reads the time, 8:35 a.m. She can make it, but she still feels a sinking disappointment at how often she's running late this week. Once is a mistake, but twice? And not only that but she also left the office early without notice.

She whips out of bed and hurries to get ready. *This is one time I'm thankful for my super speed.* Nietta gets ready in record time.

Of course, the new CEO has to come in and changed everything. Ted, her last boss, never held a meeting before noon. He was so laid back and chill, a behind-the-scenes type of guy.

As she shoves her keys into her purse, she is reminded of the guy she ran into on her way out of the office. What was his problem? She doesn't remember if he was someone from the office, she barely got a good look at him in her rush to leave.

Hopefully, he was just passing through, a solicitor perhaps. Or worst case, it was a client who now has a very jaded outlook on their services. She groans, deciding that it's best not to overthink it. She'll just run herself into a ditch with all of these jumbled thoughts.

At least she's got the energy today to deal with any setbacks. She slips into her burgundy pumps and slides her hands down the sides of her plaid pencil skirt. Her hair cascades down her back in curls and she's got her signature burgundy lipstick. Confident in her appearance she lets out a final huff, ready to face the possible backlash of yesterday's events.

———

When Nietta arrives at the office, it is just a little past nine a.m. Arriving at the conference room, she is relieved to notice that her team members are still standing up, greeting the new CEO. She straightens out her beige, plaid blazer and mixes in with the rest of her colleagues. The person in front of her takes a step to the side and she finds herself staring straight at the new CEO. Hunter Wright.

She lets out an audible gasp, unable to contain herself, and a few glances are thrown her way. She tries to play it off as the space between them decreases and the rounds of handshakes finally land on her turn.

Face to face with her ex-boyfriend, she lays notice to his deep blue eyes that always used to give her a sense of comfort. The same blue eyes that she made eye contact with after rushing into someone on her way out of the office just yesterday. *Oh fuck*, she thinks as she realizes what she had done.

Robotically, Nietta stretches out her arm to shake his familiar, large, rough hand but he doesn't move an inch.

"So glad you could join us. I do hope that we will avoid any tackling incidents today." His tone is cold and straight to the point.

Nietta can feel her cheeks warm up as she searches for his indifferent gaze. It's as if not a single trace of the past that they shared remains. He is clean-shaven, with no trace of any beard and Nietta thinks of how she used to hate it when he shaved. She preferred the beard as every time he shaved, the moment the stubble started to grow in she would get beard burns when they kissed.

"I expect a high level of professionalism from our senior agents," he says before turning to face the rest of the team, all of which have already found a seat at the table. It is a passive remark that is directed toward her. The words stung. "Right, let us move on to the focus of this meeting."

Nietta can hear Samantha snickering in the background as

she slides into the only seat available, closest to where Hunter is standing. She drops her purse onto the floor and tries to get comfortable in her chair as she ignores the hole Samantha is drilling into the back of her head. She can just feel the smug look plastered all over her face.

Samantha is a little bit of a snake. Scratch that, she is a snake. Nietta loathes how she creates an atmosphere resembling high school in the office. It's as if she just can't leave the days of being a mean girl behind.

Her first week at the office, a little over a year ago, Nietta had found Vanessa crying in the bathroom. She had explained to her how she had seen Samantha making out with her boyfriend in his car, parked right outside her apartment. Nietta had comforted her and from that moment on Vanessa had stuck to her like glue. Nietta decided that she would avoid Samantha at all costs.

It was probably Nietta's cold approach toward Samantha that grated her nerves and played on her insecurities, leading her to find any chance to try and compete with Nietta. Good thing Nietta had no potential love interests in the past year, seeing as it was Samantha's favorite sport: stealing men.

But now with Hunter in the office, she felt a sinking feeling that Samantha's watchful eyes might catch on very quickly to their rocky dynamic and find pleasure in the possibility of starting a fire.

Hunter's voice drones on in the background of Nietta's thoughts as he goes over the last stats of the last quarter and points out the areas in which he would like her team to improve. It's been a year since Nietta has seen Hunter and she couldn't help but notice how much he had changed.

The Hunter she knew was caring and charismatic. He never took himself too seriously and was always goofing around. But now, he stood before her looking more uptight and rigid than ever. In a black suit and tie with his elegantly trimmed hair, she felt impressed at how put together he seemed. She was more used to the Hunter that would prance around her apartment in sweats and a hoodie, singing random songs into her kitchenware or urging her to do silly dances with him.

The meeting comes to a sudden close as she snaps back to reality. The others get up and gather their stuff to return to their work. She follows suit and just as she straightens up to take one last inquisitive look at Hunter, she realizes that he has already vanished into thin air.

The day flies by as Nietta sorts through an endless amount of emails that have piled up over the last few days, trying to prioritize her tasks as she goes along. She takes call after call, booking shows for the upcoming weeks and scheduling meetings with the solicitor for deals that are coming to a close. As she hangs up on her last call of the day, she feels a sense of pride wash over her. It feels good to finally get back into the routine of things and get through the work that she knows she does best without having another blood lust episode.

By the time she finishes, most of the office has already cleared out, including Vanessa. She packs up and as she is about to leave, she takes one final glance at what used to be Ted's office. The blinds are pulled down, but she can still make out some light spilling through the gaps. Hunter must still be working. She wonders what he was like at his old job, the job that he did before coming here. He wasn't working in real estate but that was the one thing he had been secretive about with her, his occupation. He never brought up work when they were together and at the time it was hard to imagine him as a businessman.

Perhaps, this is a chance to talk, now that the other employees are gone and the work day is over. They had such an awkward exchange earlier and it would be nice to be able to level things out between them if they were gonna have to continue working together.

For a moment she hesitates with her hand over the door

handle. *What if he isn't willing to talk though?* She wonders, convincing herself that if he isn't willing to talk then she'll just use the excuse that she wanted to update him on the coming week's itinerary. Ted always preferred being notified in advance of major upcoming property showings. The office felt a little more dreary without Ted. He had always brought an uplifting, go-getter energy to the space. He had been her biggest support since day one.

Finally deciding to just go for it, Nietta offers a small knock before stepping in through the door. Hunter looks up from behind his desk, which is littered with the documents he is sorting through. Behind him spans a large window through which a dark, night sky can be seen. In the far distance, she can barely make out the silhouette of the forest against the horizon. Against the backdrop of stars, Hunter looks almost ethereal like a fallen angel trying to lure her out of her comfort zone.

"Did you need something?" Hunter asks, looking at her with a blank expression. There is nothing behind his passive gaze except exhaustion which weighs heavy on his eyelids. He must be putting in a lot of work to get up to speed.

"Yes, I—" Nietta starts, contemplating whether she does have the courage to bring up their past, here and now. It was something she had thought they both had moved on from and had hoped she'd completely left behind. But, when she meets his cold stare she knows that his potential to stonewall her will still hurt. So she opts for the safer option. "I just came to give you some updates."

Hunter lets off an exasperated sigh, running his hand down his face. "Those updates can very easily be sent to me over email," he replies in a deadpan tone. Without saying anything else, he returns to his computer to continue typing something up.

She stands in place, her heart sinking into the pits of her stomach. Gently bouncing from foot to foot as she racks her brain for another excuse as to why she felt the need to come to see him.

"Anything else?" he urges, clearly frustrated at her prolonged presence.

Desperation sets in and she finally finds the courage to bring up her desire to talk. "Hunter—"

"Mr. Wright." His stern expression locks in on her like an irritated bull, ready to charge. "In the workplace, you should refer to me as Mr. Wright."

Her breath catches in her throat, and she can feel a lump growing that she can't seem to swallow. "Have I done something wrong?"

The corner of his lip twitches as he scoffs in disbelief. "I think we both know the answer to that."

"What is that supposed to mean?"

"You know what it means."

Their gazes lock. For what seems to be an eternity, they just stare at each other, neither blinking nor breathing. A flood of memories rushes in as she thinks about the last time they saw each other. How he had convinced her they were just going for a romantic walk along the Pedestrian Bridge. How he had surprised her with a romantic dinner at a nearby restaurant, taken her to the bridge afterward, and then pulled out the ring. How she had run away at the prospect of forever and the fear of spending the rest of her life lying to the one man she loves.

She finally looks away, embarrassed to have even hoped that they might be able to have a civil and mature conversation. All they do is prance around the elephant in the room without acknowledging the wounds that remain. She can't let him see how deeply it bothers her. She was the one who left, she needs to take responsibility.

"I don't know what you mean, Mr. Wright," she responds with finality and lifts her purse back onto her shoulder. She twists to the side in discomfort, preparing herself to leave.

Before she has the chance to open her mouth to dismiss herself, Hunter has pushed out of his chair and placed himself directly in front of her. She takes a step back in surprise. Her back rests against the door as he closes in on her. She loses all confidence as she looks up into his dark gaze. "Stop acting so naive," he growls, nostrils flaring as he lets out a few heavy breaths. Nietta's heart is pounding against her ribcage as her breaths have picked up speed. Her chest rises and falls rapidly which draws Hunter's attention. She can feel his eyes trace the V-neck of her blouse as the familiar scent of his cologne hits her nose. An urge to eliminate what little space is left between the two arises and Nietta can feel her heart being tugged toward him.

He surprises her again by raising his hand up and instead of placing it against the wall behind her, like she thinks he's going to do, he gently tucks a piece of hair behind her ear. He lets his hand slide down the side of her neck causing her lips to part as shivers run down her spine. She sucks in a breath, letting her eyes close at the pleasant sensation.

Suddenly his touch disappears and a breeze slips into the space he previously occupied. Her eyes fly open trying to figure out what just happened.

"Hunter—"

"Mr. Wright," he repeats himself back to the rigid pretense he has picked up.

Nietta bites her lip as her eyebrows push together in confusion. This was not the Hunter she was used to. He had never been this hot and cold with her in the past.

"Fine, Mr. Wright—"

"I think it's time you went home." He doesn't say it with urgency or with desperation but rather in a soft and slow tone, as if he were talking to a child.

She shuts her mouth tightly and finds herself glaring at him. *Why does he just refuse to listen?* "Right." She shrugs her purse back into place and drops her head down for just a second, letting the disappointment settle in. "Good day, Mr. Wright."

She slinks out of his office and heads home without looking back. How is she going to be able to ignore her feelings for him now that they will be spending every working day together?

CHAPTER 3
HAUNTED

The late summer sun drenches Nietta's kitchen in a warm orange glow. She had decided that she was going to keep herself busy this weekend to avoid thinking of Hunter as much as possible. Despite it being Saturday, she's found herself at the dining table going through her work emails. Her mother always used to warn her of overachieving or overworking herself when she was younger. Even during middle school, she was quite a perfectionist. She enjoys throwing herself into work when her mind is a mess.

In the background, a whirring sound picks up as her coffee machine fills up her favorite mug. One that Hunter had bought her after she spent hours staring at it in a charity shop. He always teased her about it, calling it her "grandma cup" since it looked quite antique. It is a dusty pink, floral pattern with gold trim and she has never once had the guts to throw it out, despite the memories it brings up.

As she settles back down in front of her laptop, warm mug in hand, she continues to scroll through her emails. She lays notice to the large stack of emails from potential and current clients, color coding them so that she'll be easily able to sort through them come Monday morning. She finally reaches the bottom of the list of unopened emails and to her surprise, it was sent by Hunter, late Friday night after they had that strange interaction in his office.

Nietta hesitates, knowing full well that she was supposed to avoid thinking about him this weekend. She finally concludes that she must learn to view their correspondence as strictly professional from here on out. She opens the email, which turns out to be a response to the updates that she did end up sending to him. The email reads, "Thank you for the updates." She feels a sense of relief wash over her as her muscles loosen up after realizing that she was possibly expecting yet another harsh comment. Along with relief, she can also sense a bit of disappointment which she quickly shrugs off.

Taking a final sip of her coffee, she closes her laptop and finds her mind wandering to a specific item hiding somewhere deep inside her closet. She pushes out of her chair and carefully makes her way into the far right corner of her walk-in closet. In a box that she hasn't touched in months lies a photo album that she and Hunter had assembled over the seven months they were dating.

She settles down on top of her bed with the album splayed out in front of her. She hugs her burgundy silk robe, tightly around her trying to convince herself to put the album back and find something else to distract her with. But her hands seem to have a mind of their own and before she knows it they are flipping through the pages.

She smiles as she looks at photos Hunter took of her on her 28th birthday when she had one too many margaritas and started dancing on top of the tables with Jada. When she and Hunter had gone pumpkin picking at a farm for Halloween and got lost in a corn maze. Friday nights when they would take turns cooking for each other.

She traces her fingers over her favorite candid photo of him, one she had placed into the album herself. In it, he is gazing out at the ocean completely unaware of her snapping a photo of him. He looks so blissful and happy just to be there, experiencing life alongside her. It was one she had taken early on in the relationship when they were still getting to know each other. She had been so scared that he might react negatively but instead, he had been so happy that she had wanted to keep mementos of him.

In the photo, he is wearing the same shirt he had worn the day they met. A dark blue short sleeve hangs loosely over his torso. As she closes her eyes, she can still remember the way it smelt the first time they had met.

Nietta recalls her past memories of Hunter while looking at his photos:

Nietta's feet drag across the gravel road as she slowly makes her way home. She had just gone through one of her blood lust episodes and came to her senses right as the deer, she had tightly wrapped in her arms, fell limp.

The moon follows her like a shadow stalking her in the night. It watches her every move and Nietta can't help but feel completely out of it as the guilt washes over her. There is not a living soul for miles, yet her mind convinces her that it is the stars that are judging her.

It was her mother who had sent her into this spiral. For months they had gone with bare minimum contact, and then finally she had given in and invited her over for dinner. At first, it had been just like any of their other conversations over the phone. The usual, "How have you been?" "How's work-life treating you?" "Any potential suitors?"

Then it eventually ventured into the territory that Nietta had been trying so hard to avoid.

"How are the cravings?" her mother had asked, almost innocently. But Nietta knew full well that they had had this exact conversation on multiple occasions, and it always ended the same way. In an argument.

"Mother," she had spoken calmly to try and keep the peace. "You know I don't like to speak about those things."

Her mother had watched her with those doe-like eyes, fluttering her eyelashes like an oblivious child. "I just want to know how you're faring."

Nietta had let out a hefty sigh, in hopes that her mother would drop the act and take the hint. "Please," was all she said but her mother took her lack of response as a sign to continue.

"It's just that you are a dhampir, Nietta. Cravings can be dangerous for dhampirs. Eventually, you will end up causing a lot of harm to yourself and those around you if you aren't able to learn control." Her mother crossed her legs one over the other and placed her dainty hands on top of her knees. Instantly she switched from a naive child to an all-knowing mother.

The prim and proper mannerisms did not mesh well with her free-spirited appearance. She had multiple strings of beads hanging around her neck and her hair was adorned with a bunch of different jewels, gems, and ribbons.

"I am doing the best I can," Nietta had snapped in a harsh tone, frustrated at her mother's presumptuous attitude toward her. It wasn't like she had been a very great role model or vampire teacher growing up. Nietta just couldn't wrap her head around why her mother had become so persistent in recent years about trying to tell her what to do. "It's not like I chose this life."

"I didn't choose it either," her mother scoffed, placing herself as the victim once again. "But I have at least chosen to embrace and accept the changes that were forced upon me."

"Oh, yeah. Well, that's great, I am so happy for you,"

Nietta replied, her voice dripping in sarcasm. "Perhaps you could have embraced your responsibilities as a mother just as well as you embraced your responsibilities as a vampire."

Her mother stared at her stunned, as if Nietta hadn't said that same thing many times before. "You wouldn't understand what it's like to be a mother."

"No, I wouldn't. But I at least understand what it's like to be neglected as a child."

They stared at each other for a good few seconds before her mother let out a deep breath and said, as calmly as she could muster, "I may not have been your ideal version of a mother, but I am trying to do better, Nietta." His voice was strained, like it took every ounce of her being to keep from exploding, "You really should consider coming to stay with me at the vampire community."

Nietta's eyes rolled against her will. For some reason, her mother thought that she could be happier amongst the vampires who so blatantly rejected her. The vampires saw her as an abomination, most of them just saw her as a human and many of them saw her as a weak vampire that would never learn control. "You know they wouldn't accept me."

"It would take time, yes," her mother half agreed, "but, I'm sure they would eventually come to accept you."

Nietta searched her mother's face, wondering how serious she could be. "Regardless, I have told you before that I don't want to be a vampire. I want to be human. I want to stay where I feel most human."

Her mother's face had fallen in defeat and eyes filled with desperation. "But you're not human."

"And whose fault is that?" she snapped back, returning once again to her original argument. The fighting ensued and they continued traveling in circles before Nietta felt her wrath set fire to her cravings. Before she could send her mother home, she had already run away herself, to go feed.

She had no clue whether her mother was still waiting for

her at home or not, but at this point, she didn't care. She just wanted some peace and quiet. It was as if her mother's insisting that she couldn't control her cravings made it more difficult for her to control them. In all fairness, her mother isn't completely wrong. They were both forced into this life by a sire vampire that had turned her mother while she was pregnant with Nietta. Maybe she shouldn't be so hard on her mother after all.

As she continues to trudge down the empty road, lost in her thoughts, a bright light flashes before her eyes as tires screech against the gravel. Her heart jumps into her throat at the realization that a car is hurtling straight toward her. She feels her hands hit the ground as she braces for an impact that never comes. Eyes closed; she is frozen in place trying to process what just happened.

A car door opens and shuts as a man's voice calls out to her. "Holy shit, are you all right?" In the glare of the headlights, Nietta can barely make out the large form of a man rushing over to where she's sitting on the ground. She puts up a hand to shield her eyes and is finally able to make out a dark blue t-shirt and some baggy jeans. He looks to be about five inches taller than her, so most likely around 6'1".

He scrambles over to her side and places a hand on her shoulder. She feels a jolt course through her body at his touch. Something inside her awakens as she feels a strong pull toward this stranger. "Miss! Miss, did I hit you?" It's as if he doesn't realize that he had managed to stop his car just centimeters away from her. The shock must have gotten to them both.

Nietta, still feeling a bit dazed, slowly opens her eyes to find the most beautiful blue eyes she has ever seen peering back at her, filled to the brim with concern.

"Jesus, you're covered in blood," he says continuing to scan her body for wounds, but Nietta can only focus on his sharp features, his chiseled jaw, and high cheekbones. He's got the most luscious, dark skin she has ever laid witness to. It looks like it would be so smooth and gentle to the touch. "Hello?" He shakes her softly, attempting to get her attention. "Do you have a concussion?"

She finally finds the strength to shake her head and then drops her gaze to look at her appearance. She hadn't realized how much of the deer's blood had gotten on her own clothes, and how ripped her shirt and trousers were now. Without the backstory, it is very understandable that he would think that he managed to hit her.

"It's not my blood," she says weakly, hoping to relieve some of his fear.

But he just looks increasingly more concerned at her words. "What?"

"You didn't hit me," she continues but realizes that she can't tell him the truth either. As she slowly returns to her senses she can feel her muscles start to shake. She meets his inquisitive gaze and decides that she must compel him to forget about her, even though a tiny voice in her head tells her not to, "I am gonna get up and leave. Once I am gone, you are gonna return to your car and keep driving. You are gonna forget that this ever happened."

For a moment, he just continues to stare at her in silence. She waits for a sign that the hypnosis was successful, for example, his eyes glazing over or repetition of her instructions. But, nothing.

"Are you sure you're okay?" he asks again as if everything she had just said went right over his head. "You seem to be saying some pretty strange things." He lets out a soft chuckle with some underlying worry.

Confused as to why she can't compel him, Nietta just glares at the man wondering if she should try again. But he doesn't seem to be very accusatory of her state either so maybe she can get away without having to compel him.

"No, sorry, I'm fine," she says and then racks her brain for an excuse. "I just got lost in the woods and ended up tumbling down a pretty steep hill. You nearly hitting me just added to the shock, I guess." Her explanation falls out of her mouth in one breath. She looks up at him surprised that his presence has caused her this much agitation in such a short amount of time.

He chuckles again, this time sounding more relieved, "Oh, oh that's good." This time he shakes his head in surprise and then corrects himself, "I mean… not good that you've hurt yourself but I'm glad I didn't hit you at least." His eyebrows furrow, seemingly just as confused as to why he too is so caught off guard.

They share a look before he continues, "So what's with the blood?"

"Um, right," Nietta says having to rack her brain once again for another explanation. "I may have rolled over a dead deer." She cringes at how gross that sounds and wishes she had come up with something less gory but at least it sounds plausible.

"Oh, god," he exclaims removing his hands from her shoulders. Nietta winces at the absence of his touch and decides that she wishes she had come up with a better story. "It'd be best to get you cleaned up then." His caring and gentle expression turns into a serious one as he attempts to make a game plan. "Where do you live?"

"Next to Waveland Ave…" She replies without thinking and then wonders whether she is giving this strange man too much personal information. Somehow, his presence just feels so familiar to her.

His eyes grow wide as he looks back at her in disbelief, "That's a bit away from here. Did you leave your car some-where close by?" He lifts his head to search around as if she hadn't just claimed to have come stumbling out of the woods. She can't help but think that he looks quite adorable.

"No, I just had a pretty big fight with my mother, so I just ended up running aimlessly." Her cheeks flush as she tries to provide context for her situation but wonders if it is as possible for a human to have ended up this far from home as it is for a vampire.

"Oh well, I've got some spare clothes in the car, if you'd like them and I could drive you home," he offers and then looks a bit hesitant for a second. "If you're not feeling too apprehensive about getting into a stranger's car."

She smiles knowing that she could most likely do him more damage than he ever could do to her. She stretches out her hand and says, "I'm Nietta."

He looks at her with a raised eyebrow but reciprocates her handshake. "I'm Hunter," he replies slowly.

She lets out a little chuckle feeling like she is full of energy all of a sudden, despite the events that had just transpired, "Good. Now we aren't strangers."

Hunter retrieved the spare clothes from his trunk and Nietta threw them on over her rags. Once in the car and on the road, Nietta felt a sense of comfort wash over her. The argument with her mother, the blood lust incident and nearly getting hit by a car had all but vanished into the depths of her mind. For some reason, she felt very at ease next to Hunter.

They share a short conversation but after they sink into a natural silence Hunter switch on the radio and Nietta's eyes wander over to the window. She watches as the trees rush by and then split to reveal houses behind long driveways. She takes a moment to drink in the night sky which feels so much more joyful and accepting now than it had when she was overcome by guilt. She wants to make this short interaction with this beautiful and kind man last for as long as she can.

The song on the radio switches to "Golden Hour" by JVKE and Nietta suddenly feels entirely immersed in the music. Her eyes close, and seconds turn into what feels like hours.

Without thinking, she sing along to the music, and not too long after Hunter joins her as well. She opens her eyes and as she looks over at him, she notices him stealing a glance at her with a soft smile. Almost as if they share the exact same thoughts and feelings at that second.

"You don't seem like the type of guy to sing along to songs on the radio," Nietta teases as she continues to stare inquisitively at Hunter, trying to grasp his personality.

"I'm a man of many mysteries." He chuckles and Nietta gives him an 'as if' smirk.

They finally pull up into the driveway of Nietta's home and suddenly she gets a sinking feeling, like she doesn't want to leave the car. She doesn't want to go home just yet.

"You still worried about your fight with your mother?" Hunter asks, looking at her with concern.

She blushes under his penetrating gaze and gives off a shrug. "A little bit, but it wouldn't be the first time we disagree on something." She sits up, takes off the belt, and turns to look at him head-on, "Thanks for everything tonight. I really owe you one after this."

A nervous smile stretches out on his lips as he says, "Well, if you're serious about owing me one, then perhaps I could cash in that favor right now in exchange for your number?"

"My number?" Nietta asks surprised, feeling her cheeks get even hotter than before. "Why would you want my number?"

He looks a bit taken aback at her question as if it feels like an impending rejection. "Um— well I was really hoping that I could possibly take you out on a date at some point."

Nietta can't help but laugh a little bit at the odd circumstances. To find a woman all bloodied up on the street, claiming to be covered in deer's blood, and then wanting to take her out on a date. But, she is quite relieved because she too wants to see him again. "That would be lovely," she replies, sticking out her hand for his phone. She finishes typing her contact into his phone, texts herself just so she can have his number too, and then gets out of the car.

"Do you want me to walk you to your door?" Hunter calls as she leans back down.

"No, I'm all right. Thank you though." She smiles widely as she realizes that she will see him again. "Good night, Hunter."

"Good night," he replies, smiling just as widely as her.

She shuts the door and heads around the car toward her porch. The blue and white wooden building sits neatly between two similar-looking houses. It's got three floors with two windows peeking out from the attic, a tiny porch that spans no further than the front door, and two small trees covering the front yard. If she hadn't been working in real estate, she definitely would have never come across a house like this in Providence.

She pauses at the front door, hovering the keys just in front of the keyhole as she turns around to catch one more glance at the man that came to her aid. She offers a gentle wave goodbye and then slips back into her house, to dream about their upcoming date.

The house is completely empty, all the lights are turned off, and no sign of her mother. There is an apology note left on her kitchen island with a small "Sorry for pushing you tonight" scribbled over it. Nietta pockets the note and decides to sleep on her feelings. Hopefully, in the morning she will feel a sense of relief.

After closing the photo album Nietta feels a sense of bittersweet wash over her at the memories of her and Hunter's relationship. The nostalgia makes her want to see her mother in an odd sort of way. It is a feeling that Nietta had never really acknowledged in the past, the desire for a parent to lean on. Maybe she can have a bit of hope that they have both matured now to a point where they don't have to have every interaction end in an argument.

Deciding that she will go visit the vampire community first thing in the morning, Nietta heads out to stock up on animal blood. If she is gonna be surrounded by a bunch of judgmental vampires, then she might as well be prepared.

CHAPTER 4
GHOST OF US

The car starts with a rumbling sound that matches the increasing speed of her own heart rate. Although she had been completely set on going to visit her mother last night, and she has already notified her over text, Nietta can't help but feel a slight sense of anxiety wash over her at the thought of actually going through with her decision.

Nietta twists out of her leather jacket and throws it into the backseat as she leans over to turn on the radio to cover up the thoughts rushing through her head. At least she can rest easy at the idea of getting away from Newport and Hunter for the day. She settles in for her hour-long drive as she heads over to Middletown, where the vampire community resides.

Unconsciously her hands grip the steering wheel so tight that her knuckles turn white under the pressure. She doesn't lay any notice of this however and just keeps driving, looking out the windshield but not really taking anything in. Her mind has completely gone blank with all the stress of her emotions weighing heavy on her chest.

After a while of just driving, she finally passes through a small town littered with bodegas, convenience stores, and houses. She knows she is close and to calm her nerves she absentmindedly hums along to the songs on the radio. She reaches a stop light and as she taps her nails against the wheel, she notices a familiar man crossing the street. Daniel.

She lets out a tiny groan but feels obliged to call out to him since she knows they are headed in the same direction. She rolls down the window and yells, "Daniel!" He turns around to look at her with his dark brown eyes that have always sent tiny chills down her spine. She was never able to find the capacity to view him in a positive light but maybe that was also partially because a small part of her always resented the feeling that her mother had chosen him over her. Whether it is the truth or not.

He looks surprised at her presence but checks the road for any cars before bounding on over to the passenger side and sliding in. His dreadlocks, which are tied back in a half up half down kind of hairstyle, bounce around his face as he scrambles into the passenger seat. It is very clear to see where Brenda, Nietta's mom, got her new fashion inspiration from. He's got a multi-colored cardigan hanging right below his knees, gold necklaces adorned with jades around his neck, and a black V-neck tucked into beige loose-fitted trousers.

"What a surprise," Daniel says, settling into his seat. "To see you out and about in this neck of the woods."

The light turns green and Nietta drive gently as Daniel fastens his seatbelt. "Just figured it was about time to pay my lovely mother a visit," she says with a shrug, glad that she has the excuse of needing to focus on the road to avoid making eye contact.

"She misses you, you know," Daniel says softly and Nietta can't help but tense up. He has a way of butting in where he doesn't belong. In other family's businesses.

"I know," Nietta replies curtly, hoping that he will drop the subject. There is a long moment of silence between the two as he scrambles to find anything more useful to say.

"It's quite fascinating," he finally remarks, clearly taking the hint to switch subjects. She can feel his gaze piercing the side of her face.

"What is?" she asks inquisitively, taking the bait with a pinch of salt.

"Well, the fact that you look older than the last time I saw you." He doesn't sound like he is trying to come across in a negative way, but then again vampires have always been a peculiar species.

"Probably because you haven't seen me in over a year," Nietta offers, taking a right turn. She catches a glimpse of his face in her peripheral and realizes what he is getting at. Despite being in his mid-fifties, Daniel looks quite young for his age. Scratch that. Extremely young. Although he has dyed a few of his hairs gray to seem more his age, if a stranger was to compare the two side by side, they might think they are of the same age.

"Yes, yes," Daniel agrees. "Just fascinating to think that despite being a half-vampire, you will still age and die like a human."

Nietta's heart sinks at his words. The hard part about being a dhampir is constantly remaining split between two completely different worlds. No matter which side she chooses, she will always be seen as a freak. Even if she tries to pretend to be human, she will constantly be reminded that she is—in fact—not human.

"I am still human," Nietta states, not sure who she is trying to convince. To avoid a possible objection, Nietta decides to choose the subject this time, "So Brenda's still residing with you, I presume."

Daniel finally sits back in his seat and faces forward, away from Nietta. "Uh— yes, your mother's still hunkered down with me in our lovely van." He lets off a small chuckle as if to dissipate the tension that had been building up.

The first time Nietta had met Daniel flashes before her eyes. It had been a day where her cravings were particularly bad, back in university. She had just returned home in hopes of seeking help from her mother, but instead, she had found her lying naked in bed with a strange man. That strange man being Daniel.

"Right, in your happy little vampire community," Nietta says, trying but failing to not come off sounding sardonic.

"You know you are always welcome to join us," Daniel offers, sounding small all of a sudden. Nietta can't decide whether he is hoping that she doesn't hear him or that he already knows full well what her answer is.

"Thanks, Daniel." She sighs, finally pulling up to the campsite, placed so beautifully on the coast. "I think I'll pass."

She takes a moment to stare at the view. The wide field of scattered vans and tents, protected by the canopy of the trees. The blue ocean stretches out for miles just down the street, and the few boats swaying lazily at the end of the dock. There are lots of vampire children running around screaming in joy and adults sitting around huddled in groups, drinking blood out of beer cans and laughing their lifeless hearts out. If an unknowing civilian were to pass by, they'd look at this scene and think of it as a normal, human society filled with free-spirited people. Oh, how wrong they would be.

"You know your mother wants you to come to stay with us too," Daniel says, seemingly deciding that this is the one argument worth pushing.

"Then perhaps she shouldn't have abandoned me when I needed her," Nietta says in a tired voice as she turns off the engine and scrambles to get out of the car. As far away from this conversation as possible. This was not the reason she had come all this way. To be reminded why she had stayed away for so long.

But despite Nietta's sudden exit and her slamming the door shut as a sign that she was closing off the conversation, Daniel follows after her and continues. "It was for the best Nietta. She is safe here amongst her kind. Where I can protect her and keep her safe from—" Daniel's words grow quieter as he stops himself from saying exactly what Nietta knows he has been dying to say.

"From me?" She turns to face him, raising an eyebrow. This time she doesn't shy away from confrontation. The one thing about only having yourself to rely on is that you get used to standing up for yourself, knowing full well no one else will.

"That's not—" losing all his confidence, Daniel's words continue to trail off as he grasps for a more gentle explanation as to what he meant to say.

"It is, Daniel. But I guess neither of you ever considered that if she had just chosen to stay and teach me to control my cravings instead of running away, then nobody would have to protect anyone from me," Nietta's breath comes out in heavy gasps. Her hands ball up in tight fists at her side as she tries to calm her rising anger and frustration. The silence that fills the air gives her just enough time to realize that a few of the vampires closest to the parking lot have begun to stare and whisper. She shakes off the built-up tension. She looks at Daniel straight on, "Can you just bring me to my mother?"

He stays quiet as he gives her a nod and then turns to lead the way. A few of the vampires stare and whisper as they pass through the campsite, wondering who she is. They must not get a lot of visitors around here.

They finally reach Daniel's van at the far end of the field. He opens the door and gestures for her to go inside. As she is just about to pass him through the doorway, his hand wraps around her arm in a tight grip, stopping her in place, "Listen, Nietta. We've decided to move camp elsewhere sometime next week. If you change your mind anytime soon or in the future…" His sentence drops off for a second before he continues, "I'll text you the address."

Without replying Nietta gently removes her arm from his grip and slinks into the van. Her mother is sitting on the couch right below the window, reading a book. She looks so peaceful in the glow of the sun. The light that drifts in behind creates a sort of halo around her head making her appear more angelic than she tends to be.

Without looking up from her book, her mother smiles and says, "How unexpected to see you out here amongst the filthy vampires." She seems to find some amusement in her own mocking of Nietta's behavior.

"Hello to you too, Mother," Nietta settles down on one of the dining chairs across from her mother. She notices that Daniel has left and closed the door behind him, giving them space to speak in private.

Her mother folds a corner of the page she is on and finally closes the book to look up at Nietta. Despite her mocking, she wears a bright grin on her face. At least she is happy to see her own daughter.

"To what do I owe this pleasure?" she says, eyes twinkling with curiosity.

Nietta can't help but think, *She does seem content here in her environment, full of energy.*

"Daniel told me you're leaving tomorrow," Nietta says, unsure what else they could talk about.

"Did he know?" Her mother lifts an eyebrow, seemingly unbothered at her statement. "Yes, well it's time we pick up and leave. Sometimes humans can get suspicious when there is a community of people who stop aging around twenty."

"You're not gonna ask me to come?" Nietta asks dumbfounded. It's unusual for her mother not to press her or at least try and persuade her to join them.

But, her mother just lets out a soft sigh, "I think I've understood that you will do what it is you wish to do." She crosses her legs one over the other like she always does when she feels in control. "I'm sure Daniel will send you the location."

Nietta huffs, hating that despite her mother's lenience she still finds a way to come across as condescending. "Yes, he did say that he would." For one reason or another, her mother's gaze turns into one of pity. Nietta hates that look. She turns away and gives in to silence. They've always found it difficult to hold conversations seeing as they tend to disagree on everything.

"I just hope that you know, Nietta, that you always have a home with me. You may not be aware of it all the time, but I do love you." Her mother's words make her wince as if her whole being is rejecting the words 'I love you'. Her mother has not always been so affectionate, it wasn't until after she met Daniel that she changed. Regardless of her newfound self and motivation to spread love, Nietta just can't get used to her mother trying to care for her as she should have when she was a child.

"Right, thanks," she replies, twisting awkwardly in her seat. Then decides she can't hold it in. "But perhaps if you wanted me to live with you, you wouldn't have left me."

Her mother's shoulders drop and her leg falls off the other leg to hit the ground. "Nietta." A pained look crosses her mother's face. "I can't change the past."

An apology. That's all Nietta had ever wanted, but that was the one thing her mother could never give. "Anyway," she says, realizing there is no point in pushing the subject. She had made the promise to avoid arguments today. "There is something I wanted to speak to you about."

Once again, her mother's face lights up, back to her energetic and happy self. "What is it?"

"You remember the guy that I was dating about a year ago?" she asks hesitantly, unsure if her mother would still remember.

"Hunter, was it?" her mother asks, recognition falling across her face. "What about him?"

"Well, I told you that we broke up, but I never told you that he had proposed to me and that's why I ran away." Nietta swallows, unsure how her mother will take the new information.

"Oh," is all she says.

Nietta feels a sense of surprise at the reaction but takes it as a sign to continue, "He's taken up the new CEO position at my company now and I'm not sure how to handle it."

Her mother sits, pondering for a good few seconds. before she pipes up, "How do you feel about him?"

"What do you mean?"

"I mean, do you still have feelings for him?" Her mother can be painstakingly observant at times.

"Maybe I do..." Nietta admits but doesn't linger on the thought for too long, "I'm just scared that he hates me."

Her mother seems to be treading as carefully as she can with the topic, trying to indulge in the fact that Nietta is actually opening up to her about a sensitive subject for once. "And why would you think he hates you?"

"Because he tears into me every chance he gets and he avoids interacting with me as much as possible," Nietta scrambles for an explanation, not sure if her mother will fully understand without knowing the type of man that Hunter usually is.

"Oh, darling." Her mother relaxes her shoulders as she seems to grasp the story at hand. "Of course, he's hurt. He must have loved you very much to want to spend the rest of his life with you."

"Yes, and I ruined that chance." Nietta dropped her head in shame, wishing that her mother could tell her that it would all be all right.

"That doesn't mean he hates you," her mother continues and Nietta feels an ounce of revival in the pit of her stomach. "Sometimes anger is easier to show than sadness."

The wheels in Nietta's head start turning and things finally start to fall into place. Her mother isn't wrong. She usually isn't, but Nietta just finds it hard to admit when it comes to decisions involving her. For once, she can accept her mother's words for what they are. The truth.

"You're right," she mutters but feels she must include just one last piece of information. "I love still him."

Her mother just stares at her in silence.

In comparison to humans, vampire senses are heightened to an extreme. Those senses include emotions. When a vampire falls in love with someone, they tend to bind themselves to each other in a way humans never can. Many in the vampire community refer to this as the soulmate bond, one that can never be erased. Nietta's vampire side had bound itself to Hunter and she assumes that her mother can see it too without her having to say the words. Hunter is her vampire's chosen mate.

The door behind Nietta opens. She whips around and jerks out of her thoughts. Daniel stands in the doorway with a wary expression across his face. He finds her gaze and says, "Sorry to interrupt, Nietta, but I think it's time your visit comes to an end."

She looks over at her mother and sees that her expression has darkened from its usual vibrancy. Word must have spread that there was a foreign stranger on the campsite and anxieties must have heightened amongst the vampires.

"Right," Nietta says, getting up. Her mother follows suit and offers her a weak hug. "I'll be off then."

They part ways and Nietta rushes for her car. Trying her

best to avoid eye contact with anyone. As she heads off to Newport, she can feel a weightlift off her shoulders. When she pulls into her driveway, the sun is long gone and twilight slithers across the sky. As she takes a moment's pause in her car, she can finally say that for once her mother has helped her feel like she does have some fighting will left to spare.

CHAPTER 5
LOVE ME, LOVE ME NOT

"Good morning, team," Nietta says as she enters the conference room—bright and early—coffee in one hand, purse hanging from the crook of her elbow, and her laptop in the other. "I hope you all had a lovely weekend." Vanessa follows behind into the conference room and drops the stack of print proofs on the table as Jack gets up to collect them and hand them out to the other team members. "Are these all the designs?"

"Yes. As usual, there is a color copy and a black and white one for you to refer back to," Vanessa explains and then excuses herself from the room.

"We had eight designs submitted for the ad campaign, by the marketing team, last week. So we will have a few options to go through," Nietta says as she hooks her laptop up to the monitor. Savannah is the last team member to scurry into the room as everyone gets settled in. "Right." Nietta straightens up from her laptop after setting up the presentation and smiles, excited to get down to business. "Today's meeting will be as short and sweet as possible—as I know we all have a busy week ahead of us—so we will be focusing primarily on finalizing the ad campaign for our fifteen million-dollar listing."

The team members clap, proud to be listing such a high-value property. It felt great to be doing something positive for a change after the emotional turmoil of her terrible cravings inhibiting her work performance last week and the sudden appearance of Hunter. She felt a dip in her excitement at the thought of Hunter but shook it off.

Nietta continues, "That'll be one of our highest-grossing properties that our firm has acquired to date, and we have our long-standing client Anthony Murphy to thank for refer-ring us." She picks up her own copy of the documents that Vanessa had printed out for them. "I'd like you all to refer to the property file in front of you and make sure that you study up on all specs of this house. There is a lot of information to take in, so it will be of utmost importance to set aside a good chunk of time to get familiar with the property." A few people give her a nod of approval as she looks around the table. "Great! Now moving on to the designs. If you turn your attention to the screen I will be going through the options and following up with a majority vote at the—"

Just as she is about to start the presentation, a knock sounds at the door to the meeting room. The door swings open in slow motion as Hunter makes his way into the room. Nietta can just tell from his expression that he is not in a good mood today.

"Pardon the interruption," he says, addressing the entire room. Nietta watches as Savannah, who had been previously occupied drowning out the sound of Nietta's voice and staring at her own fingernails, suddenly perks up in her seat. "I was made aware that your team was holding a meeting regarding the ad campaign for your fifteen million-dollar listing."

Nietta offers a polite smile, confused as to what Hunter

could possibly be doing here. "Yes, we were just about to take a look at the designs."

"All right," he says, settling down into one of the chairs against the wall to Nietta's left, furthest from the door. "Let's see 'em then." She notices a few confused glances from the rest of the team as she too feels a sense of bewilderment at Hunter's involvement. Ted, their old CEO, was never one to really participate or involve himself in their team meetings.

Nietta decides to just brush it off and return to her presentation. "Um, okay. So here we have the first design," she says, clicking over to the first slide. "As you can see, it is neat, clean, and straight to the point. It highlights all the feature interior aspects of the house—"

She trails off as she notices Hunter borrowing one of the prints from Jack, sitting closest to him. He flips through the pages, completely skipping through her presentation. She can feel a sense of unease bubbling inside the pit of her stomach, like she can just tell that something bad is about to happen.

"Are these really the best designs that could be generated for this campaign?" he scoffs. Completely out of line with his interruption. Hunter meets Nietta's surprised gaze with a look of utter disappointment. "This is supposed to be the year's biggest listing and you've chosen to present designs to your team that should have barely made it through the first draft? Did I not make myself clear last week when I said that I expect nothing but the best from our senior agents?"

Nietta just stares at him dumbfounded as he continues to berate her in front of her team. She had barely made it through the first design before he decided to explode. Did he really just come in here to release his pent-up anger? The entire room falls silent, and everyone is staring at them in shock. Nietta can feel her heart in her throat as her cheeks warm up. As she realizes that it's not only her own heart she can hear beating, but everyone else's too, so she decides that she needs to get out of this room.

Before she can say anything, Hunter gets up and drops the documents on the conference table in exasperation and leaves the room. She watches his large figure bound down the hall as the door shuts close.

"OK, everyone," she says in a shaky voice. She tries to swallow, taking a moment to compose herself. "I guess, according to Mr. Wright, I shall have to reconvene with the marketing team and get back to you guys with updated designs, tomorrow. Great work today."

She is unable to find the confidence to look at anyone as they silently gather their stuff and make their way out of the conference room. After heading back to her own office space, she finds herself reconsidering what had just happened. Hunter had really crossed some boundaries and she can't just let him walk all over her like that. Not in front of her own team.

She drops her stuff at her desk and makes her way over to Hunter's office. She barges in without knocking and closes the door behind her. She glares straight at his shocked face and says, "What the hell was that all about?"

He wipes the shock off his face and replaces it with one of fury. "Ms. Williams, that is a highly unprofessional way of addressing your boss."

"Oh yeah?" she retorts, feeling her blood reach a boiling point. "That was a highly unprofessional way of addressing your employee."

"That's right, you *are* my employee. I am your boss which means it is my responsibility to uphold everyone here to the highest of standards, which—if I must say it again—your work did not meet." Hunter looks at her with fury, his chest rising and falling at a rapid pace. She's never seen him get this agitated before over something so small.

"You barely even looked at the designs!" she exclaims.

"I saw enough," he snaps and then finally breaks eye contact with her. He relaxes back into his chair as he drags a hand over his face. "I think you should get back to work, Ms. Williams, instead of standing here and berating your boss like a child."

The insult comes as a slap in the face and Nietta has never felt so humiliated before in her life. She sucks in a sharp breath and straightens out. Storming out of the office she makes her way back to her desk and plops into the chair. She can hear a few of her team members whispering in the background as she feels their stares piercing her from all angles. She closes her eyes, upset that she let him get to her. She doesn't like fighting with him, it is far more draining than it is fighting with her own mother. Perhaps because she knows that she is the root cause of all his pain.

The cravings continue to eat away at her as she cycles through an emotional rollercoaster. Fortunately, she made sure to bring an emergency stash of blood with her to the office. She pulls out the unassuming tumbler and gulps down as much as she can to relieve her thirst.

Just as she lowers the tumbler down from her face, she sees Vanessa walking swiftly across the office toward her. She closes the lid and wipes her mouth just in case any of the blood gets on her lips.

"You okay?" Vanessa whispers as she approaches her desk and leans down. Her smile fades as she studies Nietta's face. "Oh god, you look pale."

"Yeah, just Hunter… I mean Mr. Wright really stressed me out this morning." Nietta covers up for her bloodlust and offers a one-shoulder shrug.

Vanessa gives her an understanding look and says, "Yeah, some CEOs can be really nasty sometimes. The power just goes straight to their head." She makes a gesture of expansion around her head trying to lighten up the mood.

Nietta smiles at her friend's supportive words. "Yeah, yeah you're right…" she trails off, realizing that for once she doesn't want to keep brushing Vanessa off and actually try and let her in, just a little bit. "The truth is—" She meets Vanessa's inquisitive gaze with a stern one. "You cannot tell this to anyone."

"Got it." Vanessa nods vigorously. She mimics the action of locking her mouth shut and throwing the key away. "My lips are sealed."

Nietta relaxes, but still feels a small sense of embarrassment at what she is about to reveal. She leans closer to Vanessa and Vanessa follows suit. "Hunter and I... we used to date."

Vanessa's eyes grow in size, but her mouth stays completely shut.

Nietta takes it as a sign to continue, "About a year ago, he proposed to me and... I said no. I sold my house, transferred jobs, and moved out here, all so that I could get away from him."

Vanessa's jaw hangs open as she processes the information that Nietta just offloaded onto her. "You used to date Hunter Wright? Our CEO?" she says, finally finding her voice again.

Nietta looks around, really hoping that nobody is feeling extra nosy today in the office. "Keep your voice down, V," she says, flustered.

"Sorry, sorry. Just..." Vanessa trails off then quickly lowers her voice to whisper, "You know there is a rumor going around that he used to be a former CIA agent."

"Where'd you hear that?" Nietta says, surprised. If it's true then that would be news to her too.

"You didn't know?" Vanessa asks, leaning back in confusion. Nietta just shakes her head. "I mean, did he tell you what he did for work when you two were together?"

Nietta thinks back to all the times that Hunter had to blow off their plans for "work" and the many times she tried to get a clear answer from him. But, his occupation was a whole mystery that she never got the chance to unpack. "No," she replies after a moment's pause.

"So, the rumor could be true," Vanessa says, a sense of pride washing over her face at her investigative skills.

Nietta can't believe that after only a couple of weeks, Vanessa has been able to uncover something about Hunter that she was never able to. She feels a slight pang of disappointment hit her chest at the thought.

"Regardless, I can't believe you would say no to marrying that." Vanessa throws a thumb over her shoulder, directed at Hunter's office. She gives Nietta a what-were-you-thinking look and then shakes her head. "He's like a walking Calvin Klein ad. On top of that, he is a possible former CIA agent *and* a current CEO." Vanessa pauses for dramatic effect before exclaiming, "Girl, you're real crazy for that one!"

A few of their colleagues whip their heads around in their direction. Vanessa covers her mouth and looks around muttering, "Sorry."

Nietta just rolls her eyes and says, "Yeah, well I had my reasons."

"Which were?" Vanessa presses and Nietta quickly realizes her mistake.

"I uh—I just wasn't ready yet," she says and looks away. She's never been good at holding eye contact when she is lying, and it is clear from Vanessa's face that she notices.

"Right," Vanessa says crossing her arms but doesn't push any further. "So what now? Are you guys just gonna keep chewing each other out until one of you gives in or are you guys gonna sleep together? Because it is very clear to see that sparks fly every time you guys are in a room together."

Nietta looks at Vanessa with disbelief. "No, V. I really hurt him. I think what you're seeing is his explosive hatred toward me."

Vanessa scoffs. "Oh honey, I don't know what you're seeing but from my perspective, he very clearly still has feelings for you." She playfully pokes Nietta's shoulder and then throws a glance toward Hunter's office. "Besides, if he was ready to propose to you just a year ago, there is no way that those feelings have just completely disappeared. Hatred isn't the opposite of love, it's indifference."

After her wise advice, Vanessa takes leave to return to her work. They had spent a good chunk of time conversing, and Nietta has a whole pile of things to do.

The disastrous events of this morning continue to eat away at Nietta as she tries to get back into the flow of work. She spends the rest of the day communicating with the marketing team about redoing the ad designs and collaborates with a few colleagues to get various inputs. She is taking no chances in getting another vicious rejection from Hunter tomorrow morning.

The day passes and by the time everyone has gone home, Nietta is still stuck at her desk nitpicking at every aspect of the new designs. Despite being a supernatural creature, Nietta finds herself completely worn out by the stress. Even then, she continues to work tirelessly, perfecting every little detail.

She stretches her arms over her head, dropping her head from side to side trying to loosen up the knots in her muscles. She hears a scuffle down the hallway and looks up to find Hunter standing outside his office, facing her direction. For a moment he stays in place, before making his way over.

Nietta doesn't move an inch as she tries to figure out what he could possibly be approaching her for. As he reaches her desk, his eyes flicker down to her exposed abdomen where her shirt is riding up. She quickly drops her arms and when he looks up to meet her gaze, she can feel a flush fall across her face.

He clears his throat. "I just came over to check up on you," he says in a soft voice. She can tell by the way he avoids eye contact that he feels apologetic for blowing up at her earlier.

"I'm just finishing up the new designs for tomorrow," she answers back in a timid voice. Even though he doesn't seem to have come over to reprimand her again, she doesn't want to give him a reason to change his mind.

"Nietta, I'm—" he presses his lips together, hesitating to find the words. Her eyes flicker to his throat as he swallows, and she is reminded of how it used to feel with her lips pressed against his skin. "I'm sorry." The words pull Nietta out of her stupor and as their eyes meet once again she can see genuine remorse in them. Her heart softens.

"Oh, that's OK," she replies slowly, unsure of what the appropriate response is to her boss apologizing to her. "You were only doing your job, which is what I too am trying to do right now."

"Yes, but I shouldn't have spoken to you the way I did. I was worked up and…" his words trail off as his eyes scan Nietta's workspace. The garbage is overflowing with empty coffee cups, prints of trashed designs with notes scribbled all over them scatter her desk, and her hair lies in a messy bun on top of her head. She is almost certain that her face looks like a raccoon at this point with all the rubbing of her eyes she has been doing. "The designs weren't terrible. I was too harsh on you, and I should have listened to the presentation you had prepared and given you constructive criticism instead of letting my anger get to me," he wears a face of worry and distress as he rambles on. Nietta looks at her computer screen, at the hours of work she has put in fixing the designs that he ripped into this morning.

"Seriously?" Is he backtracking on everything that he already said? "I spent the whole day stressing out over these designs because you told me they were shit!"

He looks stumped at the unexpected reaction to his apology, which makes Nietta's blood boil even more. *The damage is already done,* she thinks, and then quickly simmers as she realizes that that applies to her rejection during his proposal as well. She instantly regrets having said anything.

"I think you should call it a day, Nietta," he says in a

gentle tone and lifts his hand to place it on her shoulder, but instantly pulls it away. "I am sorry for causing you this much stress. But, I do trust your expertise and I believe that whatever you submit tomorrow will be more than enough."

After having calmed her nerves, Nietta decides to put it behind her and nods ,"Okay." Hunter has been such a mystery lately that she can't help but feel constantly on edge in his presence.

After packing up her stuff they get in the elevator together and walk out to the parking lot. Just as they reach her car and are about to say goodbye, Nietta notices that her vehicle looks a bit lopsided. Her eyes shift down to the tires and notice that one of them is flat. She groans. This really isn't her day.

Hunter notices at the same time she does and simply says, "I'll take you home."

They get into his car and as he starts up the engine, a large silence takes up the empty space between them. Like clockwork, Hunter turns on the radio, the way he always did when they were in his car and had nothing to talk about.

He pulls out of the parking lot and not a few seconds into a wave of deja vu hit Nietta as the song they sang together, the first day they met, plays over the radio. "Golden Hour." The song that makes her heart drop every time she hears it. The worst part about the song is that it is so popular that even a year later, Nietta still hears it everywhere she goes.

Nietta fidgets in her seat at the flood of nostalgia that washes over her. She wonders if now is the right time to try and start a conversation with him. Maybe after fighting all day, they can try and have a civil conversation once.

"Why did you come here?" she asks the first thing that popped into her head.

He shifts uneasily in his seat and Nietta thinks that maybe he is just gonna try and avoid the conversation altogether. But, he finally answers with, "There was an opportunity for employment, so I took it."

"What happened to your old job?" she pries, hoping that he will let her in, even if just a little bit.

His body goes stiff as a sort of discomfort falls across his face. "It just wasn't a good fit." His voice is calm, but Nietta can see a vein popping out on the side of his neck the way it always does when they venture into a topic he doesn't want to elaborate on. She can't help but think back to the rumor that Vanessa mentioned, as it seem more and more plausible.

Nietta realizes that he won't give her a direct answer and she feels that it would be unfair of her to pry any further when she, herself, can't be honest with him about her own secrets. As they pull up into her driveway, Hunter parks behind her car. She gathers her purse and untangles herself from her seatbelt. As she is about to thank him for the ride, Hunter locks the car doors from the central lock. She looks at him confused but he only continues to stare straight forward.

After a moment of suspense, Hunter finally finds the courage to speak, "Why did you leave? That day I proposed…"

Nietta can feel her heart rise into her throat as a strong sense of guilt and regret wash over her. "It wasn't you," she says weakly scared to possibly hurt him all over again.

He whips his head toward her, giving her an expression of exasperation. "Nietta, please." She sucks in a deep breath, knowing full well how cliche that sounded.

"I know how it sounds, but it's the truth," she tries to convey how genuine she is being through her gaze. "It was never anything you did. You were the most perfect person I had ever met. I didn't leave because of you, and I need you to know that."

"Then why? I need to know why." He stares at her with desperation. Desperation for closure, desperation for answers, she just isn't ready to give.

"You deserved better. I just can't give you the type of life you want." She breaks eye contact as the shame fills her up.

The vampire inside Nietta calls out for her mate, yearns for her to tell him the truth, and even the human side of her wishes to give in and let him in. But Nietta's mind won't let her heart win. She must protect Hunter. She must protect herself.

"And why wasn't I allowed to make that choice? Why don't I get to choose what I deserve?"

"Because you don't have the whole truth!" Without thinking Nietta raises her voice in exasperation. She feels like she is stuck in a losing battle like a caged animal. She wants nothing more at this point than to run away. Hunter must have locked the doors because he knows her so well. To the point where he could predict her urge to run when things get difficult.

"Then tell me the truth. Give me the choice," he says softly reaching for her hand, but she pulls it away. If he touches her, she will melt.

He sighs, realizing that there is no way to get her to give in. At least not right now. "Can you just tell me one thing?"

She doesn't reply straight away, not willing to make him any promises that she can't keep.

"Did you ever love me?" his voice cracks, shattering her heart into tiny pieces. She feels the tears build up and has to muster every ounce of resistance in her body to hold them back from spilling over.

"Of course," she says finally. "Of course, I loved you. I—" her head drops as she cuts herself off before she can say 'I still love you.'

He sits back in his seat, a sense of defeat hanging over him like a rain cloud, "Right... loved." Nietta can hear the doors unlock but despite wanting nothing more than to run away, just a few seconds ago, she can't find the will to go straight away.

"Maybe love just wasn't enough." She opens the car door and gets out of the car to feel a rush of cold air slap her in the face. The sting of the chill against her wet cheeks makes her more aware of her current state of pain. She doesn't look back, afraid that if she does, she won't be able to stop herself from jumping back into the car and backtracking on everything she just said. She continues forward into the night with her veil securely draped over the monster she hides away.

CHAPTER 6
RUNAWAY

Nietta's feet dangle over the side of Hunter's bed as she faces the window lost in thought. In the background, she can hear Hunter scrambling around to get all of his things packed for the weekend. Her eyes travel to her own small suitcase at the side of the bed, glad that she had sorted everything out before she came to stay the night.

"Hey, you okay?" Hunter asks, placing a warm, gentle hand on Nietta's shoulder.

She finds his fingers with her own and says, "Yeah, just feeling a bit apprehensive."

He moves to kneel in front of her. His eyes are so reassuring and full of care that Nietta can't help but feel guilty for feeling this way. "What are you worried about, baby? It's just my family. They won't bite."

"I know…" Meeting his family doesn't scare her, but staying the whole weekend with them does. What if she can't control her cravings? What if she loses all control and accidentally hurts one of his family members? She would never be able to forgive herself.

"It's just a weekend away. Think of it like that. We've been together for six months now. My parents have been dying to meet you." His face lights up with excitement which causes Nietta's heart to bloom. Just the thought of how ecstatic Hunter is to introduce her to his family, makes her feel so blessed. "Plus, it's Thanksgiving and for them, it's so important to be with family. My parents could not stand for me not to bring you after I already told them you weren't gonna celebrate with your mother."

Moments like this are when Nietta truly appreciates Hunter's presence. He always knows exactly what to do to calm her worries. Hunter's palm caresses the side of her jaw causing her eyes to close as she leans into his touch. He trails kisses down the side of her neck that she's left exposed after tilting her head. He stops, lips hovering over her collarbone as she tries to catch her breath.

"What do you say, Nietta?" His voice is sultry sending an explosion of butterflies through her core. She lifts her head up to face him and wraps her arms around his neck. "You feel a little less nervous now?"

"Yes," she breathes as she bats her eyelashes at him. A huge smile spreads across his face as he pounces on her, tickling her entire body. She erupts into screams of laughter, happy that Hunter goes to such extent to make her feel better. The birds outside continue to chirp as they cuddle for a few seconds. In the space of their words, filled only by their heavy breaths, Nietta sends out a small, mental prayer that she won't mess this up.

He plants one last kiss on her lips as he gets up to finish getting ready. "I love you."

"I love you too." Nietta beams as the sunlight pours in through the window and basks her in its warm glow.

———

Before they left, Nietta made sure to pack as many emergency blood bags as she could. She even went as far as drinking a few in the bathroom before they left. The blood sits heavy in her stomach as she stands in front of the door to Hunter's parents' house. She switches weight from one foot to the other, hands fidgeting against the handle of her suitcase as she tries to calm her nerves.

She scans the outside of the house as she waits anxiously for his parents to answer the door. They live in a small, two-story cottage in a small village just a bit away from her home-town. It's got a small wrap-around porch that is covered in plants and wooden chairs—all different styles—scattered around for seating. There is a welcome mat in front of the sage-colored door that simply reads "welcome." She can't help but think how ironic it is, considering one of the myths about vampires is that they can only enter a house after being welcomed in.

Suddenly a few voices can be heard from behind the door and Nietta's heart jumps into her throat. It is finally happening; she is finally meeting his family. She can't help but think back to when Hunter first met her mother just a month ago and assumes he must have felt the exact same way she feels now. Though Hunter has always been quite charismatic and sociable, perhaps he found it a lot easier than she does.

The door swings open to reveal Hunter's mother. Nietta can't help but think how gorgeous she is with her glossy black curls, full lips, and eyes as dark as the midnight sky.

"Oh, it's so good to finally meet you!" she exclaims as she pulls Nietta into a hug. For a second Nietta is caught off guard, but she returns the warm gesture. Nietta is surprised at how short she is, considering her son towers over her like a skyscraper.

She smiles as his mother pulls back and she feels relieved at how friendly and welcoming she is. "It's lovely to finally meet you too, ma'am," Nietta gushes as she feels her cheeks warm up.

At the sight of Nietta's slight embarrassment, Hunter exclaims, "Ma, please don't scare her away."

His mother shoots him a quick glare before turning back to Nietta. "It's Jemima, dear, but you can call me Jem." She offers Nietta a small wink before turning her head over her shoulder to shout into the abyss of their house. "Brandon! The kids are here."

The sound of heavy footsteps bounds down the hallway around the corner. A tall, burly man with an olive skin tone walks into the foyer. Nietta can finally see where Hunter gets his height and bright blue eyes from. He stretches his hand out toward Nietta as he squeezes in beside his wife. "Nice to finally meet you."

"You too, sir," Nietta replies, feeling all her nerves return once again. She wraps her hand in his and finds herself nearly dragged down by the heavy grip. His lips stretch into a wide, satisfied smile and Nietta can only thank some of her vampire strength for surviving that handshake.

"Go easy on the girl," Jem says, smacking Brandon in the side to which he only responds with a chuckle.

"Her grip might be stronger than mine," he teases as he lets go of her hand. If she had gone full vampire on him, she would have been stronger than him.

Hunter shoulders his bag as he grabs Nietta's suitcase and navigates around his parents into their house. Nietta follows suit as Jem ushers her inside. Once in the foyer, Nietta finally notices a young girl who looks to be around nineteen. Hunter had shown her many pictures of his sister before, but she was definitely more adorable in person.

"I'm Robin." She scurries over with her hand stretched out. She is nearly as tall as Nietta and wears a plaid dress with black leggings underneath. Her hair is pulled back into a neat ponytail, tied off with a lilac bow. She looks so prim and proper.

"Nice to meet you." Nietta smiles, reciprocating the final handshake of the evening. "I'm Nietta." As their hands grasp in a gentle shake, Nietta feels just a slight sense of dizziness. For a moment she thinks she smells blood, but quickly shakes it off. She just fed not too long ago so it shouldn't be a problem.

"I hope you won't mind sharing the room with Robin?" Jem pipes up as she follows Hunter down the stairs.

"I've left your bag in her room, already." Hunter gives her a warm smile very clearly doing his utmost to make her feel comfortable and welcome.

Nietta responds with an expression of appreciation and says, "Of course, Jem. I wouldn't mind one bit."

As his parents scurry back into the kitchen to continue preparations for dinner and Robin goes into the bathroom to finish off her make-up, Hunter decides to show Nietta around their house. With a gentle hand on the small of her back, he guides her down the upstairs hallway which is lined with photos of him and his sister as children.

He points out Robin's bedroom and then leads her into his childhood bedroom. Every piece of furniture and decor inside the room looks like it's frozen in a moment of a time long gone. The walls are painted a baby blue, there are posters of random bands scattered across the walls and photos of Hunter and his high school friends. The shelves on the walls carry basketball trophies and some stacks of video games.

The bedroom isn't big and there is merely a single bed, which Nietta assumes is the reason she will be staying in his sister's room. He did mention how they had fought for ages when they were younger about who would get the large bedroom, once their parents had finished renovating it. Robin had won the rights to the room after a simple match of rock-paper-scissors. Prior to that, they had both been stuck sharing the same room for six months.

"This is me," he says, waving his hands around. He spins to face Nietta as he drops his arms to his sides and sits down on his bed. "My parents haven't gotten around to getting rid of the childhood mementos, seeing as they are so sentimental and all."

"It's cute." Nietta glides her fingers carefully across his photos and trophies. "Gives me a glimpse into the old you."

"The old me." Hunter chuckles, taking a glance at the photos she's staring at. "Can't say the old me was as impressive."

Nietta shakes her head and walks over to Hunter. "But the old you is the reason for the current you." She places her hands on his shoulders, feeling much more comfortable now that they have a second alone. His eyes fill with excitement as he grabs hold of her waist and guides her onto his lap.

"Is that so?" his voice is husky as she brings her lips down to meet him. They share a deep, long kiss before she pulls back.

"How long do we have before your mother's expecting us for dinner?" she asks, watching as Hunter's eyes glaze over in passion. A small tingle crawls down her spine.

"About an hour," he whispers, lifting his hands up and under her shirt. She can feel his warm hands grip firmly at the sides of her ribcage over her bralette. For a moment her eyes close as she relishes his closeness.

"Then I will have to excuse myself." Her voice is small as she tries to pull herself back out of her lust for his touch. His hands slide back down to her waist as he leans in to plant a few gentle kisses along her collarbone. "It'll take me about an hour to get ready."

Hunter groans and gives her skin one final kiss before removing her from his lap, "Fine, princess, but you sure know how to tease a man."

She smirks, running her hands over his hair before slipping out of his room and into Robin's. Seeing as Robin is still in the bathroom, Nietta takes it as a chance for a moment of peace. After all the introductions and the prospect of sharing a long Thanksgiving dinner with Hunter's family, she can't help but feel on edge. The butterflies and nerves cause her cravings to become just a tiny bit harder to control, but a moment away from the chaos allows her to find a sense of balance once again.

She fishes out her toiletries bag and places a blood bag inside to keep in the bathroom in case of an emergency. As she waits for Robin to finish up, she slips into a knee-length, long-sleeve, beige jumper dress. She drapes a gold necklace around her neck to finish off the look.

————

"How was the drive, sweetheart?" Jem asks as Braydon heads into the kitchen to check on the turkey. They are all finally sat around the dining table mostly lit by candlelight as the main lights have been dimmed for ambiance. An orange runner divides the table in two, with tiny white pumpkins and two cinnamon stick scented candles scattered up and down the runner.

"It went smoothly," Hunter says curtly before looking at Nietta, seemingly asking her telepathically if there is anything she wants to add.

"Did you show Nietta the rose farms by the fire station? The blooms are beautiful right about now," Jem continues oblivious to their little exchange.

"We haven't been to the farms yet, but I plan on taking her there on the way back," Hunter replies, taking a small sip of his water before adding, "Nietta did mention that she was quite enamored by the woods just outside of town."

His gaze finds hers as he gently sets his glass back on the

table. Nietta smiles, knowing that he is trying his best to bring her into the conversation. "Oh yes, the forest looked absolutely gorgeous."

Jem looks slightly surprised by Nietta's choice of noteworthy scenery before returning to her enthusiastic 'travel advisor' persona, "You must take her on a walk there someday then."

Braydon calls out from the kitchen that the turkey is ready and Jem motions for everyone to grab their plates.

"Sorry, I'll be back," Robin mutters to her mom as they all get up from the dining table. Jem gives her an understanding nod before ushering the rest of them into the kitchen. As they crowd around the food, Jem explains all the different dishes they have prepared and finishes with, "Help yourselves, please."

Nietta follows Hunter's lead and is just about to plate some cooked Brussels sprouts when Braydon yelps out in pain. Nietta can smell it before she sees it. Blood. She whips around at the same time as Hunter to see that Braydon had managed to cut himself while cutting into the turkey.

"Sorry, sorry," Braydon mutters, rushing over to the sink. "It's just a minor cut," he reassures everyone as he washes up the wound. Jem hurries to get the first aid kit as Nietta's heart races.

"You okay?" Hunter asks as he wraps a hand around her arm. "You've gone real pale."

His words jumble together as Nietta feels the cravings take over. There is a warm pulsing sensation filling up her gut as the vampire inside of her demands to be released.

"I—" Nietta gently pushes Hunter's hand off of her as she tries to come up with an excuse to leave. "I suddenly feel really dizzy…" She mumbles her words not exactly sure what she is trying to say as she rushes out of the kitchen and up the stairs.

Without thinking Nietta rushes into the bathroom and

finds Robin standing by the sink. She looks up at Nietta surprised at the sudden intrusion. The smell of blood hits her again like a slap in the face and Nietta notices a box of tampons on the sink next to Robin.

"Sorry," Nietta says as she looks at a wide-eyed Robin.

"No, it's OK. I should have remembered to lock the door," Robin says in a reassuring manner. The same kind of comforting tone that Hunter always uses with her. Nietta takes a few clumsy steps backward as the smell fills her entire mind with thoughts of feeding. Feed. Feed. Feed.

"You okay?" Robin asks, straightening out. Her look of surprise has morphed into one of worry. "You really don't look good."

Nietta can't process what Robin is saying nor can she make any sense of her thoughts. All she knows is that she must get out of there before she does anything she will regret. Deciding to forget about her emergency stash of blood bags, Nietta runs out of the bathroom. She races down the stairs past Hunter, who is coming up to check on her. In her haze, she is able to remember that Hunter hung up the car keys on a hook, next to the front door. She grabs them before making her way out into the chilly night and into his car.

She recalls taking note of a blood bank on their way to Hunter's family home, a few miles out. Once at the blood bank, she wastes no time sneaking into the facility and finding her way to the blood bags. Her vampire has almost taken over and due to the cravings, it's like the whole thing feels like a dream. Back in the car she chugs down two bags and falls apart in the driver's seat.

Everything went by so quickly and now that she's finally replenished her thirst, she can't help but feel a wave of shame wash over her. There is no way that she can come up with an explanation right now and she most definitely doesn't want to have to go back and face Hunter and his family. Afraid that they might start a full-on interrogation, Nietta decides that she will find a motel to stay the night in.

After having a shower and laying down on top of the bed like a starfish, it's around midnight when Nietta hears a knock at the door. Confused, she looks through the peephole to see Hunter standing right outside. How did he manage to find her?

Not wanting to make him wait outside in the cold, Nietta opens the door despite only being dressed in the motel's bathrobe. "What are you doing here?" she asks in shock as she takes in the state of her boyfriend standing right outside her motel room. His chest rises and falls rapidly, his hair—which is so short that it's difficult to ever mess up—lays in a mess on top of his head, his eyes are full of worry and concern, and his clothes are lopsided with his hoodie on inside out.

"My friend owns the motel," he says in between quick breaths. "I—he called, said he saw my car parked outside. He thought that maybe it had been stolen."

The fear on Hunter's face makes Nietta's heart sink even further. She caused this. She caused him all this pain and confusion just because she couldn't control her bloodlust. "I'm sorry," she says in a small voice, scared that he might blow up at her, scared that the events of tonight have caused him apprehension toward her. What can he possibly be assuming from tonight's events?

He doesn't say anything but instead just pulls her into a tight hug. They stand there for a good few minutes before pulling apart. Nietta steps aside to let him into the motel room and they take a seat on the bed.

"What happened tonight?" Hunter's wide eyes search hers frantically, looking for answers that she doesn't want him to find. She can't take the pressure of eye contact and instead looks away. She fidgets with her bathrobe while she tries to rack her brain for an excuse. "Hey." He places his hands on top of hers in a comforting manner, trying his best to gain back her attention. "You know I love you and I'm here for you no matter what it is you are going through."

She finally finds the strength to meet his comforting gaze and can't help but melt in those warm blue eyes. There's a sense of home and familiarity in Hunter that Nietta has never been able to find in anyone else, not even her own family. He brings her so much trust and honesty that it tears her apart knowing that she must keep lying to him.

"I have diabetes, Hunter." The words spill out of her mouth before she can stop herself. It's not that far off considering her cravings do have to do with the condition of her physical being. She lulls over the idea in her mind and for a second she is even able to convince herself that it could be true if she was human.

His face falls in sympathy as he wraps his hands around hers in a tight grasp. "Why didn't you tell me earlier? Why have you been hiding that from me for so long?"

She pulls her hands away and stands up, feeling agitated at the questions he's begun to fire at her. The hard part about lying is making it all connect. If just one thing seems off, the whole story falls apart. "I was embarrassed," she says, hoping that the less information she gives the less he is able to see through her.

"Embarrassed about what?" He stands up too and tries again to comfort her with physical connection by placing his hands on her shoulders and turning her gently to face him. "There is absolutely nothing for you to be embarrassed about. It's not like it's something you can control, or you chose to bring upon yourself!"

The words hit home as Nietta realizes that despite not knowing the actual truth, the words are still somewhat applicable to her situation. She gives in to his touch and leans into his arms finding comfort in his healing words.

They stay the rest of the night in the motel room together

with Hunter taking care of Nietta, bringing her a cold wet towel every thirty minutes and rubbing her back as they watch TV. Despite his kindness and despite him voicing his unconditional love, Nietta can't shake the growing feeling inside the pits of her stomach that he would be better off without her.

————

A few weeks after the incident with his parents, Hunter texts Nietta to get dressed up since he has made reservations for them at a nice restaurant near Downtown. In those few weeks, Nietta's worries had only continued to grow and by the time dinner ended and Hunter led her to the Michael S. Van Leesten Memorial Bridge, it was starting to dawn on her what his true intentions were.

He pulls out a bouquet of flowers and a few pedestrians stop to stare as he gets down on one knee. The whole world starts spinning as reality comes crashing down. In his mind, she is his forever. But she will never be able to let him see the real version of her without facing the inevitable truth that a dhampir can never be with a human.

She mutters a simple "no" before running, and she never stopped running ever since.

CHAPTER 7
TELL NO LIES

"You'll do great," Vanessa reassures as Nietta gathers the printed documents that she hands her. She hasn't felt this nervous since the first client she took on on her own. But knowing that this deal has been a huge talk in the company as of late makes her feel like it could potentially make or break her entire career.

"Thanks." She rolls her shoulders back and straightens out as she drags her sweaty palms down the sides of her tan, knee-length skirt. She's got a black turtleneck tucked into her skirt, a tan blazer to match, and black leggings underneath to compliment the black shirt. Her black heels click-clack against the floor as she makes her way back to the conference room.

As she waits for the client, Nietta continues to run through the slides and her notes an endless amount of times. She feels the words start to jumble together into a huge mess in her mind as the more she goes through the presentation the more she forgets where it started and where it ends. In the background, the ticking of the clock that hangs on the back wall of the conference room grows louder and louder. Her heartbeat fills her ear canals with an increasing rate that causes her head to spin.

In a last-ditch effort to control her rampant emotions Nietta closes her eyes and quietly counts down from ten under her breath. As she reaches one, her phone buzzes in her pocket, and without even looking, Nietta knows it's an alert from Vanessa that the client is standing at reception. She hurries out of the conference room and is surprised when she takes in the appearance of her client. Her mother used to always tell her that "assuming makes an ass out of you and me" and as Nietta approaches the client, she can't help but feel that there is no phrase more fitting at this very moment.

"Hello, you must be Mrs. Johnson." She smiles as brightly as she can as she stretches out her hand, aware of all the curious stares of her colleagues piercing into her back. Seeing as the reference was Anthony Murphy and all she had was a name, Nietta had the assumption somewhere back in her mind that the client would be an old lady looking to sell property inherited by a late father. Instead, before her stands a young woman who looks to be somewhere in her late twenties to early thirties. She is dressed head to toe in Chanel with a platinum blonde bob peeking out from under her pink plaid hat. Nietta finds herself almost surprised that there isn't a poodle peeking out from her shoulder bag.

"Yes," the woman says in a dull tone as she eyes Nietta's hand. She is frozen for a good minute before Mrs. Johnson finally gives her hand a swift shake.

"Right this way," Nietta says, doing her best to keep up her confident persona. She leads Mrs. Johnson through the office and into the conference room. For the first time ever, she finds herself analyzing the environment. The floor-to-ceiling windows that look directly over the water does offer a sort of luxurious feel. Perhaps something that Mrs. Johnson will appreciate.

She pulls out a chair and gestures for her to sit. "Please, make yourself comfortable." Mrs. Johnson slides into the open seat without a glance at Nietta nor a single expression of gratitude. "Could I offer you some coffee, tea, or water?"

She merely throws an uninterested look at her wristwatch and Nietta can't help but feel thrown out of kilter at the icy mannerisms of her client. She clears her throat as she straightens out and decides that Mrs. Johnson is unintentionally rushing her. *Hopefully, she will just accept whatever I present to her*, Nietta thinks as she concludes that Mrs. Johnson most likely has no interest in the whole process whatsoever.

"To get started I will be running through what we have prepared for the ad campaign." Nietta starts the presentation and finds herself in a comfortable lull as she presents everything just the way she had practiced. By the end of the pitch, a sense of pride washes over her. "Any questions?" She turns back to face Mrs. Johnson and finds her completely disinterested. Somewhere during the presentation, she had pulled out a nail clipper and started fidgeting with it. Nietta's heart drops into her stomach as she wonders if the client had been listening at all during her speech.

"Murphy really did give your company way too much credit," Mrs. Johnson says as she clips the air next to her fingers with the clipper. She shakes out her bob as she lifts her head to give Nietta a strong look of disappointment. "I can't say that your presentation has managed to reassure me of your talents. Quite the opposite, actually."

The words float around in Nietta's mind as she finds herself frozen in place. This was the first time that she had faced such a harsh backlash from a client. Never once had she failed a pitch and this was the most valuable listing of the year.

In the space of their words, Mrs. Johnson mutters, "Disgraceful," under her breath as she accidentally cuts herself with the clipper on the way out of her chair. She hisses and then as she makes her way to the door, she throws her head over her shoulder and says, "I expect much better the next time I waste an hour out of my day to come all the way down here." Then she disappears out of the room, leaving behind a distraught Nietta who can focus on nothing but the lingering smell of blood.

With her emotions caught in disarray, her usual guard has been dropped and the tiny speck of blood that Mrs. Johnson left behind sends her over the edge. Just as she rushes into the hallway she rams face-first into a sturdy chest, that smells like Hunter. As her senses heighten, she picks up on all the separate conversations going on throughout the office at the same time. She feels the noise and the smells hit her like tidal waves as she cringes against the sudden intrusions of her perception.

"Hey, what happened?" a voice calls out to her from above and instead of looking him in the eye, she shoves past. While straining to restrain her vampiric strength and speed, Hunter is able to catch onto her wrist just as she is about to break for the bathroom. "Nietta, I asked you a question." His voice sounds serious as he tries to control her urges to run away.

But it is already too late. As he whips her back around to face him her eyes have already started to turn black, and she can feel her fangs protruding out of her mouth. His eyes widen in shock. In the pits of his blue, swirling eyes like never-ending skies, she thinks she detects a flash of disgust quickly masked by fear as he takes in her true form. She goes completely numb as she rips her arm away, utilizing her full strength. She vanishes out of the office as she realizes that there is no turning back now.

———

For the next couple of days, Nietta refuses to leave the house. After the horrifying meeting with the client and the even more horrifying encounter with Hunter, she can't bear to pull herself out of bed. The only time she left the house was to stock up on blood and to go to the hospital to compel her doctor to write her a doctor's noteworthy enough to excuse her from work for at least a week.

Once again, she has found herself avoiding all the texts and calls that Vanessa has been bombarding her with. She even received a few messages from Hunter that she couldn't even bear to imagine what they said. Perhaps he's expressed utter disgust, perhaps he's put together all the pieces in his head and figured out the truth all on his own.

Her spiraling thoughts keep her in an endless loop that continues regardless of whether she tries to focus on something else or not. Her fears keep her on her toes as she goes for runs, or tries to watch shows. Every time she attempts to put her mind to something else, she finds herself spacing out and forgetting about how much time is actually passing.

It's around dinnertime when she finds herself sprawled out on her tiny two-seater couch in the living room. Arms and legs dangling off the sides as if someone has just dumped her there and left. Her eyes wander the crevices and marks on the ceiling trying to muster up the energy to come up with something to make for dinner.

As the sound of a clock ticks slowly in the background, the shock of the doorbell ringing pulls Nietta out of her stupor. She feels her heart sink as she racks her brain to figure out who it could possibly be, but she is interrupted by the bell ringing again.

She whips off of the couch and as she opens the door slowly, she finds Hunter standing there with a bag in hand.

"I brought your favorite meal," he says as he lifts up the bag. She searches his face for any signs of hostility or disgust, anything that would tell her that he knows. Why would he come here though if he knew what she was? "Look, I think you and I both know I deserve some answers."

There it is. He wants the truth and this time she knows he won't take no for an answer.

"Come in."

CHAPTER 8
UNRAVEL

The silence befalls them like a friendly shadow that has followed them since the moment they met. It sits heavy on Nietta's shoulders as it awaits the truth that she has hidden for so long, for the words that lie on the tip of her tongue and have threatened to come out many times. Her fork clinks against the plate as she reaches for her glass. Her throat parched from the impending doom. She can no longer escape, and she has used up all the excuses in the book. Even if there was an excuse left to give, Hunter has already seen her for what she is.

"Nietta," he says, pulling her out of her thoughts. Her eyes land on his thin silver chain that hangs just centimeters above the tabletop as he leans in to grab her attention. "You're gonna have to say something."

But she doesn't want to speak. This is the one thing she has wanted to avoid for ages. The moment she tells him, what will he think? He'll see her for the monster that she truly is. Perhaps he will be the one running this time and she won't have the energy to chase him. It will be over for good. The coffee machine screams in the background and comes to a gurgling stop as her homemade cappuccino sits waiting. She's frozen in her place at the table as her eyes detail the carvings on her utensils. She is so focused on avoiding a conversation that she doesn't notice Hunter getting her coffee for her until it is placed in front of her on the table.

"Speak," he demands in a gentle yet firm tone.

Surprised by his impatient command, Nietta snaps her head up to face him. He lets off a huge sigh as she gives him her fearful, doe eyes. *This is it*, she thinks as he throws himself back into his seat, *I have to say it*.

"I'm a dhampir," she mutters as his face twists with confusion.

"A what?"

"A dhampir."

He intertwines his fingers together as he places his hands on the table. "I have no idea what that means," he says slowly as if he too is scared to push her away. As if his urging for her to explain will cause her to give up and leave, again.

"It means—" she takes a huge breath preparing herself for whatever is to come next. "It means that I am half-vampire half-human."

"How?" he asks trying to find the right words to say, the right questions to ask. "How did you become dhampir?"

Nietta takes a big breath as she prepares to dive into the miles-long explanation, "It's a long story, okay?" She pauses. "It happened when my mother was pregnant with me. She was just eighteen, kicked out of her house, and had nowhere to go. My father wanted nothing to do with her, so she was left to fend for herself. After weeks of living on the street, some random guy offered to take her in. He said that in exchange for help around the house, he would give her food and a roof over her head. At that time, she was desperate enough to risk it, so she went with him. He gave her everything he had promised but as soon as she had gotten comfortable, he bit her and turned her into a vampire. My mother and I believe that the reason I was born as a dhampir was that the vampire venom that turned her into a vampire latched onto my DNA in her womb. As I wasn't directly bitten, it was only powerful enough to make me half-vampire."

For a moment he just stares at her, processing everything she has just told him. Then his expression changes as if a light bulb has gone off inside his mind. "It sounds so outlandish when you say it," he starts, fidgeting with his chain, "but it would explain a lot of incidents."

"Like the fact that I don't have diabetes?" She chuckles lightly trying to loosen up the mood. The tension is suffocating her, but it feels awkward making light of someone else's ailments. Her smile drops as she returns to the carvings in her utensils.

"Yeah... to be completely honest with you, I knew that was a lie." Hunter shrugs, giving a little jostle of his head. "I just didn't want to push you. I never wanted to push you, but I always held onto the hope that you would come to me with the truth on your own."

Nietta feels her shoulders drop as surprise washes over her. "You're not upset?" Hunter's reaction is so different from what she had expected that she can't help but feel taken aback. To her, it feels like having been in an elevator plummeting toward the ground only for it to stop on its intended floor and she realizes that it was all in her head. There was nothing to fear.

"Mad?" He moves his hands closer, reaching out for her in a way he hasn't done in a long time. She grabs hold of his fingers and meets his loving gaze. "I've always told you that I would love you no matter what. If this is your reality, then I will accept it with my full heart."

"No, Hunter," she whispers as she pulls her hands back to her side. Her head drops. "Look, just because I told you the truth about what I am, doesn't mean that anything can change. It just means that now you know why I can't be with you."

His facial expression grows darker as confusion falls across his face, once again. "I don't understand. Why can't we be together?" He gets up and crosses the floor to her side. "I know the truth now and I've said I will stay. Isn't that what you were so afraid of? That I would reject you?"

Nietta shirks away from his gaze, feeling suffocated by his closeness. The urge to run away builds up in the pits of her stomach as she tries to calm her nerves. "Yes. I was afraid that you would reject me for being a dhampir, just like everyone else has. But the reason I never told you is that knowing the truth wouldn't change the reason I have to stay away." She finally turns to face him, and she sees all the emotions of desperation, fear, and sadness flash through his eyes. Not only was her true identity dumped on him but so was the fact that there is still a gap that exists in their bridge. A gap that they will never be able to fix to cross over to each other's side. They will forever be staring longingly across that unfixable hole

.

"Why do you have to stay away?" His voice is soft, slowly vanishing into the space between them. She can see it in his body language, in his tone, he knows there is nothing more he can do to change her mind.

"As a dhampir, I am unable to control my cravings like a full vampire can. I have a weak side and a strong side. I would be a constant threat to you and if we were to ever have kids in the future, most likely they would be just like me, and I don't want that. I would never wish this life on anyone else." Her voice cracks as the explanation flows out of her like a river breaking through a dam. This is it. The end of the truth. She wraps her arms around herself as she feels naked and exposed.

He notices her shaking and pulls her into a tight hug. For

a moment they stay there drinking in each other's warmth. *This feels like goodbye,* she thinks. But then he pulls back just slightly and caresses her cheek as he leans in for a kiss. She quickly places a hand in front of his lips.

"Hunter, I—" she can't bring herself to say it. She doesn't want to be alone, but this is the right choice. "I think it's time for you to go."

Pain. His whole expression twists as if she's just stabbed him and as his mate, she can feel that pain just as deeply. She hates pushing him away. Over and over again. She hates it.

"Right," he mutters, and then without another glance, he disappears out the door and into the night.

A tear falls down her cheek as she sinks out of her chair and onto the floor. She curls up into a ball as she feels the chill take her. It's as if her heart has been ripped out and as her only source of warmth, she can no longer produce any more body heat.

He has completely unraveled her and now she can't find the strength to put herself together again.

CHAPTER 9
ALL GOOD THINGS

Before the sun has even had the chance to peak above the horizon, Nietta is in her car and on her way to the vampire community. After her conversation with Hunter, she finds herself desperate for advice and the only person she can go to is her mother.

She arrives at the location that Daniel sent her to, which turns out to be a nearly empty parking lot in the middle of the forest. There is a path for cars leading further into the forest and she can only guess that's where the campsite is. She decides to call him up and see if he can come to meet her there.

"Hello?" his voice comes over the receiver. He always sounds so surprised whenever she interacts with him.

"Hi, Daniel," she replies, gently closing the car door behind her. "I'm at the location you sent me but all I see is a gigantic forest."

"Right, don't worry. I'll come to get you." A beeping noise follows after he hangs up and Nietta can't help but sigh. Her mother and Daniel just really detest the idea of her showing up amongst the vampires unaccompanied.

It takes a good few minute for Daniel to show up, and a good few minutes for which Nietta spends staring at the tree tops trying to make out the clouds passing by above the canopies. It is hard to see anything beyond the trees looming over her which makes her feel so small and insignificant. How anyone could enjoy living this isolated life is far beyond her. Perhaps I'd be a fool not to consider isolating myself seeing as I don't belong in any community, she thinks to herself.

Daniel finally appears down the broad path leading into the woods from the parking lot. He raises a hand in greeting as he comes into view. "I'm glad to see you've made it."

He stops in front of her awkwardly as she keeps her arms tightly wrapped around her torso, "It was a long drive but I'm here now." She sways slightly from side to side as she feels the awkward silence crawling in.

Fortunately, Daniel is able to avoid the silence by clapping his hands. "Well, let's get you to our camper van then, shall we?"

They trudge down the dirt path in silence as the campsite appears out of thin air. It's placed neatly in a large opening in the forest with tents, vans, and cars scattered all about. There is a small building for bathrooms, grilling, and a few picnic tables under cover. It looks almost as if they just picked everything up from the last campsite and placed it down here, exactly as it was. The only difference Nietta can see is the scenery.

Once again, a few of the vampires stare as they pass but Nietta avoids eye contact. She really doesn't want to raise suspicion again. This time, as they approach the van, her mother is sitting outside in a beach chair with a sunhat on and a book in her lap. She smiles as she sees Nietta approaching and gets up to pull her into a hug.

"Let's go inside," she urges as they pull apart and Nietta nods.

Inside she accepts a cup of tea as they settle down into the seating area. Her mother wraps her hands around her knee as she always does, prepared to listen and say her piece.

"What's brought you out here?" she asks curiously as she continues to smile at her daughter. It hasn't been that long since they last saw each other and even Nietta is surprised at herself for coming all the way out to their new campsite. At first, she had thought it redundant of Daniel to send her the address, but instead, she found herself using it sooner than expected.

"It's about Hunter," she begins as she fidgets with her floral midi skirt.

"Oh?" Her mother's eyebrows raise in surprise. It's not often that Nietta opens up to her mother about her love life, so of course it seems unusual for her to bring it up so often. "What about Hunter?"

"Well, there was an incident at work, and he saw my fangs. I avoided coming to work for a few days, but he showed up at my house and demanded that I tell him the truth. As my mate, I can't compel him, and I had no more excuses left so the truth just came spilling out." Nietta breathes heavily as the whole story rushes out of her in one breath. She can't find the courage to look her mother in the eyes, afraid of what she will say.

"He's quite stubborn, isn't he?" Her mother chuckles.

She wasn't expecting her to take the news so lightly, especially since she hates involving humans in the vampire world. "I guess so." Nietta lets out a sigh of relief and then finds herself giving in to a little grin. She never really thought about that before, but Hunter truly doesn't seem to know when to give up. Despite her lying to him for so long, he did say that he held onto the hope that she would one day tell him the truth. Which she did… after a little bit of a push.

"It just doesn't change anything." Nietta sighs, feeling the sadness take over her again. Her mother moves to a seat closer and stretches out her hand to place it warmly on top of Nietta's.

"Unfortunately, the mate bond won't let either of you walk away from the other." Her mother reaffirms what Nietta already knew to be true deep down. What is supposed to be the blessing of a true life partner, has turned into a curse that she can't escape.

"I just wish that I wasn't a dhampir," Nietta says as all her muscles let go of the strain of holding her up. She doesn't have the energy to sit up strong and tall anymore as she curls up into a ball on her chair. "I wish there was a way for me to just be human."

Her mother sucks in a sharp breath and responds, "Be careful what you wish for darling." She lets go of Nietta's hand and falls back in her seat. "Sometimes we just have to accept reality for what it is and learn to make the most of it."

They part ways as Nietta returns home. As she pulls up in her driveway, she notices a figure standing on her front porch. They turn around at the sound of her car and she realizes that it's Hunter. What is he doing back here again? Didn't their last conversation make things more clear for him?

She slams the door behind her and jogs up the driveway as he comes to meet her halfway. "What are you doing here?" she asks as he grabs onto her shoulders.

"I have found it," he says between excited breaths, his facial expression lit up with exhilaration. "I've found it!" he repeats one more time as his grip on her shoulders gets tighter.

Confused, she grabs onto one of his hands in hopes of getting him to lighten up his grip. "What are you talking about?"

"The cure." His eyes pierce straight into hers as if he were trying to telepathically send her all the information that he had just supposedly discovered.

Nietta rubs her temple as she tries once again to get an explanation. "Hunter, you're gonna have to elaborate."

He finally lets go of her shoulders and starts making grand gestures as he explains, "I started researching last night after we spoke and I got really into it. Eventually, I came upon this article that claims that there is a way to turn back into a human after being bitten by a vampire."

Suddenly the world spins really quickly as Nietta's heart races at Hunter's revelation. Is this true? Could she really have the possibility of fulfilling her dream of getting rid of her vampire half? For a moment she just stood in place trying to process what Hunter had just told her. On one hand, it feels too good to be true but on the other hand, Nietta just wants some inkling of hope to hold on to.

"Does it explain how it's done?" she asks, still feeling incredibly skeptical.

"No…" Hunter trails off and it's like a shot to the heart. Of course, it was too good to be true. "But, I've got the address for the shaman who wrote the article."

Oh? Nietta thinks as she lights up once again. "Oh?"

"Yes." He smiles clearly proud of himself. He wraps his hand around the back of her head and leans in to kiss her forehead, "I'll pick you up first thing in the morning and we can go together. Right now I think you need some rest."

Nietta nods in agreement as her thoughts continue to pass through her mind at miles a minute. There is a lot she needs to process before she feels that she will be ready to go see this mysterious shaman.

CHAPTER 10
COME TO AN END

"Are you ready?" Hunter asks as they pull up in front of a small shop in Downtown Providence. He turns off the engine as he leans over to Nietta, eyebrows raised as he tries to gauge her mood from her facial expression. She traces the lines in his forehead with her eyes, the slightly crooked trail of the bridge of his nose down to the peaks of his cupid's bow. She gives him a soft reassuring smile as she turns back to the partially dilapidated wooden shop in front of them. The crooked sign, barely hanging on to the roof by its rusted chains, reads "Yama's Crystal Shop." Is this where they will find the answers they have been looking for?

She gives him a soft, reassuring smile and then turns to scan the area. They are at the edge of Downtown Providence, back to the state they both grew up in. By the time they've arrived, it's a little past noon and the sun hovers above them. As her eyes close, she imagines how much more pleasant the warmth of the sun will feel on her skin. How less intense the world will be to experience as a human.

"I'm ready," she says, closing her eyes for a split second

and taking a final breath. They get out of the car at the same time and hesitantly approach the vacant-looking shop. Hunter reaches the door first and holds it open as Nietta enters before him. Inside the lighting is dim and the air is filled with the strong smell of incense which blooms inside Nietta's nasal canals and fills her head with smoke. The counter is lined with jars full of a variety of different colored crystals and jewelry. The wall to the far left is lined with books and from a few Nietta can make out the titles: *Reiki Healing for Beginners,* and *The True Art of Meditation.*

They maneuver around a couple of round tables taking up space in the middle of the floor as they make their way to the young girl standing behind the counter. When she looks up Nietta is met with two hazel orbs that look like swirling pools of molten lava when the light reflects directly into them. Her black hair is trimmed at the sides of her head and short on top. It flows into a smooth curve toward the right side of her head and Nietta guesses that she looks to be around twenty-three years old. She wears a necklace made out of a shoestring with a silver star made out of paperclips. Her navy, plaid blouse is buttoned up to mid-chest revealing a black tank underneath, and is rolled up to just above her elbows.

"Can I help you?" she asks as Nietta and Hunter stand at the counter. With a raised eyebrow she bounces her gaze between the two as she waits patiently for their request.

"I—" Nietta stumbles over her words as her skepticism bubble up to the surface. Maybe they were wrong and maybe this was the wrong place. Maybe the shaman who wrote the article is no longer alive. It's as if the whirlwind of thoughts makes it difficult for Nietta to focus on her objective.

"We're here looking for Mr. Yama," Hunter speaks up as Nietta lets out a relieved breath, thankful for his presence. She doesn't know if she would have managed to get the words out on her own. Perhaps she would have just been shooed away after spending a good few minutes just standing there, opening and closing her mouth like a fish out of water. "He wrote this article." Hunter pulls out his phone with the article still open in his web browser. The girl rises onto her tiptoes as she leans across the counter and squints to read the words.

"That would be my great-grandfather," she finally says, settling back onto the balls of her feet. "He wrote that ages ago. What could you possibly want to know about the article?"

Hunter and Nietta share a quick glance before Nietta quips, "We wanted to know if it's true." This statement earns her an amused look from the girl. Nietta can sense that she isn't fully human herself, most likely she retains divine powers like her great-grandfather. "Is he here?"

The girl gives a slight nod and says, "You're in luck. He's usually out on some fishing trip with my dad but maybe he had a feeling you'd be coming." A small shiver runs down Nietta's spine at the notion of this old man being able to predict the arrival of a stranger whom he's never met. The girl must notice the slight discomfort flicker across Nietta's face as she lets out a slight chuckle, "Don't worry, I was only joking." She scurries out from behind the counter and through another door at the backwall.

For a moment she vanishes out of sight, but Nietta can still hear her as she calls out for her great-grandfather. A raspy voice responds and a flurry of voices echo behind the walls— a middle-aged man's voice, an old woman's, and a middle-aged woman's voice—before they can be heard shuffling toward the door. The girl reappears with an old man hanging onto her left arm. He hobbles across the floor to one of the tables and as he leans onto the wooden surface, the girl hurries to grab him a chair from behind the counter.

As he settles down he lets out a gurgled groan and then twists in the direction of Hunter and Nietta, who have been frozen in place during the entire fiasco. "I heard someone was asking about an old article of mine?"

Hunter springs into action as he moves over to the old man's side. He whips out his phone once again and says, "This one. You wrote about a ritual that can turn a vampire back into a human."

The man wiggles his thin, gold-framed glasses out of his breast pocket and onto his nose. He leans closer to the phone to try and get a better view of what Hunter is trying to show him. Then as if a lightning bolt went through him, he jolts back. "Ah yes!" he grumbles as Nietta moves to stand next to Hunter. "I can't believe you've dug up this old bugger." He chuckles as he looks at them from over his glasses. "What exactly is it that you want me to answer?"

Hunter clears his throat as Nietta can feel a small squeeze inside her gut. This is it, either he tells them it's a complete scam or that there actually is a way, and Nietta doesn't think she can handle any more disappointment. "Is it true? Is there a way to perform this ritual?"

The old man frowns. "There is a way, but it depends on what your circumstance is. How did you get turned? Who turned you?" The old man seems to point all his questions at Hunter which doesn't surprise Nietta as he is the one doing most of the talking. He must not have a way of telling vampires from humans. This is the first time that Nietta has ever met a warlock so it's interesting to have an idea of their abilities.

Nietta finally decides that she has to take over the interrogation, seeing as it is her issue they came here to discuss. "I'm a dhampir," she says, taking a gamble on whether they are vampire friendly or not. The old man and girl have now both placed their full attention on Nietta, and neither of their facial expressions has changed. They continue to stare blankly, patiently waiting for her to elaborate. "My mother was pregnant with me when she was turned, and the vampire venom had spread to my DNA making me a half-vampire."

The old man just nods gruffly before pulling out a bag

from his jacket pocket. He tips it over the table and pours out a handful of bones. He closes his eyes, takes a deep breath, and throws the bones on his exhale. He does this repeatedly before he finally says, "I am being told that the answer to your question is—yes, you can get rid of the vampire venom..."

Nietta feels her heart swell inside her chest. This can't be real. This can't be happening. She feels the world start to spin again as the thrill of achieving the one thing she's always wanted becomes more and more real.

"But..." her heart stops, "you may not find the solution as pleasing as my initial answer."

"What do you mean?" Nietta asks in fear as she feels Hunter's warm hands grip her shoulders, trying to provide her support in light of potentially bad news. "I came all this way for the truth, be it good or bad," she insists as she notices the shaman hesitating to reveal the final part of his answer.

Finally, he shakes his head and says, "To be rid of your vampire curse, you must get rid of the source that made you a vampire."

"And that would be?" Nietta asks even though she knows exactly what he is getting at. She can feel it coming before he says it.

"You must kill your mother," the shaman states as he closes his grip around the bones and shuts his eyes as if consulting the spirit world one more time. He drops his head and places the bones back into the bag. "That seems to be the only way."

Nietta feels the world tilt as it comes to a sudden stop from all of its spinning. She rocks on her feet as she falls into Hunter's strong grip. He steadies her, leaning into her back with his firm torso. She falls apart as the realization hits her like a train. The one thing she's wanted more than anything else and the only way to get it is to kill her one and only family.

"I can't do that," she mutters.

"I understand dear, unfortunately, that is the only way for you to become a human again," he answers.

"So, I'll just have to stay the way I am," she whispers, still in shock. "I'll just have to be a dhampir for the rest of my life."

An uncomfortable silence falls over the group as Nietta finds herself swept away by a hurricane of despair. She feels all her hope fly out the window as she stares into a bleak and barren future.

Hunter and Nietta thank the shaman and his great-grand-daughter as Hunter leave his contact information if they come across anything else. They exit the store together and for a few minutes, the two of them just sit in silence as they try to process the information they have just been given. The sun has begun its descent toward the ground, signifying to them that it's time to head home before they get stuck crossing states in the middle of the night.

The ride home is silent as Nietta continues to stare out the window lost in thoughts. She feels an ache grow inside her chest as her thoughts ramble on. Why is life so unfair? Why can't anything good come without consequences?

CHAPTER 11
BOUND

Nietta bursts through her front door with Hunter following close behind. She paces around her kitchen as she tries to sort through all the emotions and thoughts, she's kept pent up inside during their drive back.

"I can't believe that this cure gets dangled in front of my face like a carrot on a stick," Nietta throws her arms out as she vent into the open air, "...and for that cure to be killing my own mother?" She scoffs as she abruptly stops in her tracks and smacks a hand against her chest. "Someone must be playing a sick joke on me right now."

"Nietta," Hunter tries to take on a soothing tone as he slowly approaches her. "Maybe we should take a deep breath and try to talk this through in a calmer manner," he suggests, which causes a fire to start within the pits of Nietta's stomach. Unknowingly, Hunter has just stepped right on top of her minefield and right on top of a mine.

"Oh, don't you dare patronize me right now." Nietta shoves a finger in Hunter's direction as she bares her teeth.

She can feel the edges of her fangs sticking out just slightly as her emotions flail around like a rollercoaster. It's so hard to keep the vampire at bay when she's lost control of her own emotions. Now that he knows, she doesn't even bother to conceal the struggle between her vampire and human form.

"I'm not trying to patronize you," he says and when he realizes that he has his palms up, facing her like you would toward a child he quickly drops his arms to his sides. "I merely want to help, but I can't do that when you're throwing a tantrum."

"A tantrum?" Nietta screeches as all she can see for a hot second is red. Then she is back to her human form as she can feel the sweat start to form in droplets at her temples. "I'm not throwing a fucking tantrum; I'm having a breakdown because I'm crushed."

"I understand," Hunter says, "I'm just thinking that maybe if we talk about this, we can fix it together."

"Fix what? There is no way to fix it, Hunter. I—" Nietta finally let's go of the rage and gives in to the sadness that washes over her like a single wave. A wave that doesn't drag her down but merely makes her feel wet, cold, and miserable. "I can't do it," she says with finality as she stares intently at her feet, "I can't choose you over my mother's life."

Hunter takes a step in her direction as he reaches for her arm, "Nie-" Before he can finish, she is gone. She rushes out the door using her super speed and into the woods. She keeps running until she feels a pang of heat that knocks her to her feet.

Nietta screams in shock at the pain as she curls up on the dirt floor, arms wrapped tightly around her stomach. What the hell is going on? Sweat pools under her armpits and runs down her back. Her skin feels as if someone has set it on fire and her mind is warped beyond comprehensible thoughts.

After what feels like an eternity Nietta can make out a figure of a person lurching toward her in the darkness. She can hear a voice calling out to her, but it sounds like someone trying to scream underwater. All of her sensory perceptions have become distorted as her body is forced to fight off a sudden onslaught of pain.

As she sweeps in and out of consciousness, she can feel someone picking her up and carrying her at one point. The next time she is brought back into awareness she is lying in her bed, with someone holding her hand. The next time she comes to, the birds are chirping, and a warm breeze filters in through her window along with the morning sun. She groans as she lifts a hand to the wet towel draped across her forehead. It feels warm to the touch, but she assumes that at some point it was cold, intended to bring down her temperature.

"You're awake?" a voice calls out from the door, and she looks over to see her mother standing there, hands resting on either side of the door frame. She's got a white, flowy, long-sleeved top draped across her torso and a ruffled, black, floral, midi skirt. She makes her way across the room to where Nietta is lying on top of the covers, closest to the window.

The covers below her body feel wrinkled and moist as Nietta places her hands down to push herself up into a seated position.

Her mother rushes over and places her hands on Nietta's arms to give her support. "Slowly, you've only just woken up from your fever," her mother says as she helps Nietta lean against the backboard.

Nietta lets out a deep groan as she feels the aftermath of the fever that wreaked havoc on her body. "What happened?" She rubs her forehead, unsure what exactly happened to her.

"You're experiencing something we vampires refer to as mating fever," her mother replies as she settles into the chair next to Nietta's bed. She must have been using it while she nursed Nietta back to health.

"Mating fever?" she asks, completely lost as to what her

mother is talking about. She knew that vampires subconsciously form mate bonds, but she had no idea that on top of that, they had to mate? What are they, bunnies?

"It means that you and Hunter have not yet completed your mate bond," her mother explains as Nietta cringes at the idea of being nearly thirty years old and having to have a similar conversation as 'the talk' with her mother.

"I don't like where this is going," Nietta begins, and her mother just shakes her head.

"It's not just that, it's about both parties fully accepting their responsibilities as each other's mates. You must perform a ritual in order for the bond to be completed, otherwise, you will continue to be stuck in limbo." Everything her mother was saying to her felt like she was speaking a whole other language. She just can't wrap her head around what she is getting at.

"So if we don't give in to the mate bond, I will be stuck like this?" she asks as it dawns on her what her mother is saying. This could be real bad. Yet another burden she will have to carry.

"Most likely," her mother says quietly as she watches Nietta with a look of worry.

They both sit in silence for a good while until Nietta finally speaks, "I guess there's nothing I can do about it right now then."

"Nietta," her mother sounds frustrated, "it will only get worse and worse. From what I have heard there is no way of getting out of a mate bond. You are tied together for life and the more you try to reject it the more it will force you to subdue."

Nietta's head spins once again and as she goes to lie down her mother scooches closer as her eyebrows crease in worry. "I'm ok," Nietta mutters as she holds up a hand to stop her from coming any closer, "I just need some space."

"You seem better now, so I will head out. But remember, I am only a call away." Her mother packs up all of her things and takes off, leaving Nietta with an empty house and a mind full of raging thoughts.

CHAPTER 12
NOWHERE TO HIDE

A couple of hours after her mother left, the doorbell rings as Nietta lies in bed scrolling through her phone. Her nose scrunches up at the thought of having to leave the comfortable embrace of her blanket. But, after the doorbell goes off a second time, Nietta is forced to drag herself out of bed.

She swings open the door to find Hunter standing there, once again.

"What are you doing here?" she asks as he shifts his weight from one foot to the other. She's not surprised that he'd want to come and check on her after the last time, but she is surprised that he timed it so well with her mother's departure.

"Your mother texted me," he replies, scratching the back of his head in a sheepish manner. He drops his gaze for a second and then looks back up into her blank stare. "After I found you passed out in the forest, I brought you back here. Funny enough, your mother called just as I was putting you down on your bed, so she came and took care of you. She told me to go home, took my number, and said she'd text me once you were doing better," he explains after having observed her curious look. She nods slowly and then lets out all the air she had been holding in.

In his presence, the strain of the mating bond sits heavy on her chest as if a whole mountain has fallen on top of her and is steadily crushing her. She can feel the invisible pull toward him, and she wonders if she will be able to stave off another wave of the mating fever. As she slows her breathing and focuses on her thoughts, the pull withdraws slightly like a negative wave.

"Can I come in?" he asks finally after a long pause.

She nods. "But only for tea. After that, I really have to rest."

The two of them sit in silence at Nietta's dining table as the kettle lets off a low whistle in the background. As the whistle increases in pitch reaching an opera-like scream, she gets up to go and pour up the tea. Hunter's phone starts ringing as the water streamlines out of the kettle and into the mugs. She hears him get up and escape into the hallway.

"Hello? This is Hunter Wright speaking."

Nietta finds it almost amusing that he hasn't seemed to fully grasp the extent of her vampiric abilities yet. He must not realize that whether he goes into the hallway or outside the house, she will still be able to listen in on the conversation.

She settles back into her chair as she leaves his tea on top of his placemat.

"Oh, I wasn't expecting to hear from you so soon." Hunter sounds shocked, which causes Nietta's intrigue to heighten. Without realizing it, she leans in closer to the direction in which he is standing as if to help her hear the conversation better. "You what? Are you sure? That's amazing! I-I gotta go tell Nietta. Yes. Yes, I'll make sure to relay that as well. Thank you, bye." As he reappears back into the dining room Nietta is hanging off her chair in anticipation. She awkwardly scrambles to get back into a more natural pose as she tries to cover up the blatant fact that she had just been eavesdropping. "Uh—" Hunter says in amusement as he taps his phone against his palm. "That was the shaman," he says, sending Nietta's heart into yet another whirlwind.

"Oh, god," she mutters, scared to give in to hope once again. "What could he possibly have to say?"

Hunter meets her worried gaze with one of reassurance as he gives in to a tiny smile. It's not a full-blown one, which tells Nietta that it isn't going to be anything like "just swallow this potion and you'll be human." She prepares herself for the worst. "Well, there is another way for you to become human without killing your mother," he says slowly.

"What is it?" Nietta asks impatiently as she stands up and moves closer to Hunter for support. But, in getting up too quickly along with the sudden excitement and nerves, the mating fever surges in like a tsunami and drags her under. A flash of light passes before her eyes as the heat spreads through her body like poison. She screams out as Hunter sinks down to the ground along with her. His arms hover around her body as if unsure of whether to hold her or not.

"What's happening?" he asks in desperation as she continues to groan in pain. "Nietta, stay with me."

He finally throws her into his arms as he rushes her into her bedroom and gently places her onto her bed. He leaves and returns with a bucket of water and a towel. He strips her down to just her underwear and gently pat sher skin with a cold towel. The last thing she sees before losing consciousness is his eyes overflowing with fear.

CHAPTER 13
INTERTWINED

Branches grab at Nietta like hands reaching out through the darkness, ripping at her clothes trying to pull her down as she races through the forest. The dirt floor sinks beneath every step she takes, and she feels like she is fighting against quicksand. Her heavy breaths fill her ears. Her head is filled with fog. Fear chokes her as she desperately tries to escape from the shadow figure chasing after her.

It calls out to her in many voices. "Nietta," it says in her mother's voice, and then again it calls, "Nietta," but this time in Hunter's voice.

She claws at the trees she passes, doing her best to push and pull her way through the overgrown bush. The night sky hangs over her like a weighted blanket as the full moon laughs mockingly at her weak plight. It taunts her from its position high in the sky, away from any danger.

Her foot catches something large and heavy on the ground as she finds herself tumbling toward the earth. Her hands land on sharp rocks as she yelps out in pain. She scrambles through the dried leaves to figure out what she fell over, and a face appears beneath the pile. A face that morphs into her mother's.

"You did this," her mother says in a raspy voice. Her disappointed tone was like a knife straight into Nietta's gut. "You did this to me." The life vanishes from her mother's eyes as she draws her last breath.

"No." Nietta whimpers as her shaking hands reach for her mother's lifeless face. "No, please. Don't go." Sobs pour out of her as she desperately tries to bring her mother back to life. Tears cloud her vision as the shadow figure finally catches up and looms over her shoulder.

"You made your choice," a voice says from behind and she whips around to see Hunter standing there. But it doesn't look exactly like him. His eyes are completely black, and his face is morphed into a vicious smile. "You killed your own mother."

"No," Nietta's voice trembles as the realization washes over her. She chose to kill her mother for her own selfish greed to be human. "No, I— I didn't want to."

The monster that looks like Hunter looms closer and closer. His mouth gapes open as if to devour her. Her screams wake her up as she lurches into a sitting position in bed.

Hunter, who had been hovering over her, dodges as she almost head-butts him. "Woah," he chokes out, eyes wide as he tries to soothe her with his gentle hands. "Hey, it's okay. You're awake."

She is still breathing heavily as she tries to take in her surroundings. Her eyes dance around her room in search of her dying mother, in search of the shadow figure. But they are all gone. The forest is gone, and she is back in her room.

"It was just a dream," she says out loud trying to calm down. "It was just a bad dream." She shuts her eyes, taking slow breaths. She focuses on Hunter's soothing hands, gliding down the sides of her arms.

"You're safe," he says in a soft tone, wrapping her in a protective hug. He continues to pat her back as she lets go of the fear that had enveloped her dream. She sinks into his body, allowing him to hold her up as her strength dissipates.

As they sit there in silence, Nietta trying to calm her nerves and Hunter trying to comfort her, a familiar tug grips tightly onto her gut. She pushes Hunter off of her, fully drenched in fear once again. He stands at the edge of her bed in complete shock at her sudden change in mood.

"You have to leave," she says, eyes wide. The vampire inside her digs his claws into her organs as it fights to be let out. She groans in pain as she tries her best to push it back down.

"What are—" Hunter starts but Nietta cuts him off.

"Now, Hunter! You have to leave now!" she shouts at him in frustration, scared that it'll be too late. The last thing she wants to do is hurt him. The last thing she wants to do is lose the one person keeping her sane.

He refuses to listen and instead kneels at the bedside, grabbing onto her hands. "Nietta, I can't leave." His eyes are full of desperation as he begs her to not push him away. "I need to stay here with you."

Nietta's chest rises and falls rapidly as she feels tears well up in her eyes. She doesn't want to push him away. She wants him to stay but she's too scared.

"No, Hunter…" she whispers through the tears as her mouth fills with the salty taste. "It's for your own good."

His grip tightens around her hands as he leans in closer, "It's too late Nietta. We are bound together, and I know you can feel it too. We can't keep running from this. From us." His eyes pierce deep into her soul as she feels the mating bond tug her toward him. She knows. Everything he is saying, she knows.

For once she can't help but give in. As she leans in toward his face, she feels her nerves tingle with joy as their breath mixes together. Her whole face flushes with warmth and her heart explodes as their lips brush together. Hunter's hand reaches for the back of her head as he deepens the kiss.

They pull apart for a moment to catch their breaths. Nietta's hand grips the front of her shirt as she tries to calm down her beating heart. All she can focus on is Hunter's strong torso pressed up against hers, his fingers wrapped up in her hair. His big, soft lips trail wet kisses down her neck and along her collarbone. His free hand slides up under her shirt and grips her breast. She feels her whole mind go blank as he pulls her head back slightly, leaving her skin even more exposed.

His fingers dance over her nipple as he bites gently into the soft skin on the crevice of her neck. She moans as his teasing sends tingles up her spine.

"I want you," he whispers into her ear as he presses into the space between her legs, "I want all of you." She melts into his strong embrace as she lets into the passion.

Their lips meet once again but this time more hungry, more desperate. The fire between them ignites as they devour each other. Hunter's hand moves from her breast, across her stomach, and down to the lining of her pants. He hovers above her skin for a second before diving into her panties. As his hand makes contact with her wet mound, she can't help but groan out in ecstasy. She has been waiting for this for so long.

He pulls his hand out of her pants and rips off her shirt as she rips off his. They start to undress each other like animals lost in their desire for each other. Between every removal of every clothing item, their lips clash together and part. Even though they have had sex together many times before, this time feels like the first time all over again.

As he hovers above her, waiting for her consent to enter, Nietta stares deeply into his gaze and can't help but feel the safest she's ever felt in ages. She gives him the nod of approval and as she feels him slip inside of her fully, she is lost in the joys of being completely and entirely connected once again.

CHAPTER 14
DEADLY DESIRES

Nietta traces the lines on Hunter's palm as they lie in silence intertwined in her sheets. She feels the pull toward Hunter has gotten stronger and knows that they are now halfway through completing their mating bond. The thought of them being tied together eternally scares and excites her all at the same time.

"There's something I wanted to tell you," Hunter says, breaking the silence between the two. She leans her head back on his chest as she peers curiously up at him.

"What is it?" she asks as his chest rises and falls soothingly beneath her.

"You remember the call I got when we were drinking tea?"

"Yes."

He peers down at her and then looks back up at the ceiling. "It was the shaman. He called to tell me that he has found another option to get rid of the vampire venom."

Nietta's heart races as the words sink in. Another option. Another chance. But, she feels the fear of being disappointed once again grip her chest even tighter. "What is it?" her voice trembles in anticipation.

Hunter hesitates as if he is worried whether she will receive the news positively or negatively. "He said that he redid his clairvoyance ritual and came up with a new answer. He realized that the true source of your vampire form isn't your mother but the vampire that turned her. The sire vampire."

The information churns inside her mind for a second as she realizes that someone must still be killed in order for her to be human, but this time it is someone to whom she has no connection whatsoever. The one who forced her mother and her into this life. The one who took away their chance at a normal life.

"Nietta," Hunter says pulling her out of her trance. "What are you thinking?" He sounds cautious, still unsure of how she is taking the news.

She doesn't know how to feel about it but at least she no longer has the idea of killing her own mother haunting her anymore. "I don't even know who the sire vampire is," she says finally as defeat washes over her. The excitement of the past hours and having to deal with the mating fever for the last couple of days has completely drained her.

She feels as if there is a deep abyss inside of her that yearns to be filled. Her cravings start to bubble up to the surface as she loses all power to fight.

"Hunter... I think you need to leave." She gurgles as she tries to hold down the vampire that is waking up inside of her.

"What do you mean?" he asks, completely taken off guard. "No. We've been over this already." He sounds frustrated and hurt that she is trying to kick him out once again. What's worse is that she is having to do it right after they made love.

"No, it's not the same," she tries to explain herself, but the vampire is rushing out of her like a volcano explosion. She feels the tips of her fangs peek out of her lips as her eyes go completely black. "Run," she squeezes out between rapid breaths as her vampire takes over.

Hunter doesn't say anything as he shoots out of the bed and out of her room right before she lunges to attack him. She moves slowly across the room as she tries to fight against her vampire. She is in hunting mode as all she can think about is the need for blood. His blood.

She is finally unable to hold back any longer as she runs rampant through the house trying to find him. All she can do is try to ignore the trail of his smell, the sounds he makes in order to confuse her vampire. As if she was hanging onto the back of her vampire trying to cover her eyes as she searches for her victim.

Please, she thinks in desperation, *please stop.*

CHAPTER 15
TO BE FOUND

The front door slams open as Nietta's mother rushes into the scene. Nietta is standing in the middle of her kitchen, eyes fully black, fangs protruding as she froths at the mouth. She has lost complete control over her vampire and is somewhere deep inside of herself screaming to be let out.

"Nietta," her mother says as she approaches her slowly, "you have to control it. You have to break free from your cravings." She has her hands up as she tries to lure her out of her trance, but Nietta is lost.

There is no coming back now, is there? She tries in vain to snap out of it. The amount of times she has tried and failed to control her vampire is endless. She feels hopeless and alone.

"I know you are in there somewhere darling. You've just got to hold on for a little bit longer." Her mother slowly approaches her. As she gets closer and closer her grip on her purse gets tighter. Her knuckles go white as she sticks her hand into her purse.

Nietta can feel her vampire preparing to fight as the

distance between the two of them closes. *No,* Nietta screams inside her head, *I have to hold back. I have to.*

Suddenly her mother whips out a syringe and stabs her in the arm with it. The liquid fills her up and causes her to go completely numb. She falls to her knees and as she places her hands on the cold, hardwood floors she feels all her strength completely dissipate.

"It's vampire venom," her mother explains from somewhere above her, "it will subdue you completely, including your vampire, for a while. Don't worry, it'll only make you weak for a few hours." Her mother joins her on the floor as she wraps Nietta in a warm comforting hug. They stay like that for a good amount of time.

In the background, Hunter reappears from his hiding spot in the bathroom. Nietta can hear his footsteps grow closer as he approaches the scene. Despite the ringing in her ears and the spinning of the room, she is still able to make out their conversation as clearly as day.

"What happened?" her mother asks as she gets up from her position next to Nietta on the floor and turns to Hunter for clarification.

"I'm not sure. One second, she was fine and the next her eyes went black, and she was trying to bite me I think," Hunter replies. The trembling of his voice makes Nietta's heart sink. She was so afraid to hurt him. He must hate her now.

"Cravings," her mother says, "the mating fever must have depleted all her energy and left her unable to control them."

Nietta can hear Hunter shuffle around a bit. "She was trying to tell me to leave but I didn't listen." He sounds disappointed in himself. She wants to scream out that it's not his fault. That it is her fault. Her fault for being this way. For being a monster.

"I'm sure she would disagree," her mother says. "You

were just trying to be there for her like anyone would for their loved one."

Nietta finally stops trying to resist the venom as she feels her vampire retreat completely into the shadows of her being. She sinks further into the ground as she stares at the crevices in between the wooden planks of the floor.

"Well, actually," Hunter starts as he prepares to tell her mother what he had just told Nietta over an hour ago, "we found out that there is a way to make her completely human."

"What do you mean?" her mother sounds surprised, almost elated at the information.

Nietta feels a sense of warmth spread in her chest at the thought of her mother being happy at the chance to fulfill her daughter's dream of being human.

"We went to visit a shaman and at first he told us that the only way to get rid of Nietta's vampire venom was to kill off the source," he hesitates before he finds the strength to continue, "which initially he believed to be you." There is an awkward silence that falls through the room following Hunter's statement. Nietta cringes at the thought of her mother realizing that she had even considered killing her for one second. "Of course, she refused. But then he called me earlier tonight and revealed that the source would actually be the vampire that turned you. The sire vampire."

"So we'd have to kill the sire vampire?" her mother says. As she paces in a small circle, stars start to dance before Nietta's eyes. "Well, good thing I know exactly where to find—"

A loud ringing shrieks through Nietta's ears and sends her into a downward spiral. The world around her swirls like a whirlpool as her body goes entirely limp. She loses consciousness once again.

CHAPTER 16
NOW OR NEVER

Once Nietta wakes up from the vampire venom her mother injected her with, she finds herself sprawled out on the couch in her living room. The TV is playing silently in the background as she turns to notice her mother sitting in the armchair next to her.

"You're awake," her mother says, sounding relieved to see that Nietta has returned back to consciousness. "These past few days have been really rough on you, haven't they?" Her mother offers her a lopsided smile as she gets up to move over to the couch as Nietta sits up to make space for her.

She groans in pain as the strain of the mating fever and the cravings come crashing down on her. "I feel so dead," she mutters as she bends over her knees, head in hand, trying to stretch out all of her tensed-up muscles. It feels as if she has just woken up from a month-long coma.

"That's probably from the vampire venom," her mother explains as she slides a comforting hand down Nietta's back. Nietta slowly closes her eyes as she relishes the moment. For a long time, this is what she had wanted from her mother—

comfort and validation. The two things her mother seemed to never be willing to give when she was a child. Maybe she really has changed since she left for the vampire community and Daniel. "I know that you're still not in top shape." Her mother hesitates whether they should speak now or let Nietta rest longer.

"What is it?" Nietta says, conveying that she is ready. Whatever it is, it seems important. She sits up straight and turns to look at her mother who drops the hand that had been patting her back. She can feel it in her bones, the time is coming. The time to decide whether she will be going through with the shaman's ritual or if she will have to back down.

"Hunter filled me in on what the shaman had told you both," her mother says as Nietta thinks back to what she had heard right before passing out. She cringes once again at the idea of her mother being informed that the initial option was to kill her. "He told me that in order for you to be human, you have to kill the sire vampire."

Nietta nods. She remembers those words coming out of his mouth but after that, she had been unable to keep up. A flurry of butterflies explodes inside her stomach as all the possible outcomes rush through her head. *What if her mother has no idea where the sire vampire is now? What if they have died? What if they have moved out of the country? What if—*

Her mother interjects her train of thoughts. "I know where the sire vampire is. I can help you complete the ritual." Her mother's eyes search Nietta's as if trying to figure out if this is what she truly wants. "If being human is what you desire, then I will do everything I possibly can to help you, Nietta." Her mother's reassurance sits warmly in Nietta's chest. For once they are no longer on warring sides but on the same team.

The words "if this is what you truly want" float around her head for a second as she considers the vampire inside of her, the vampire that has been there her whole life. Of course, there was a time before her fangs grew in. A time when she did live a somewhat normal life. Unlike most vampires who get thrown in the deep end, having to feed right from the get-go, Nietta being a dhampir had made her life much more different. Although every vampire has once lived as a human, they were all unknowing of the fact that they would one day become a vampire. For Nietta's specific circumstance, she still retains her human DNA which is what makes turning back an option for her.

She truly is fortunate. *But is it fortune or greed?* She thinks and then quickly shakes the thought from her head. Sometimes in order to be happy one must choose to be selfish. The world won't hand her happiness on a silver platter, she must make a happy life for herself. At least the life that she hopes will make her happy.

"I want to go through with it," Nietta says in a firm voice. "I want to be fully human." She looks at her mother and for a second wonders if, in a way, this is her choosing Hunter over the one who gave birth to her. Her own flesh and blood. Her mother's life will continue to be with the vampires and if she chooses the human world, will they still be able to continue the way they have?

As if her mother can read her mind, she lifts a gentle hand and caresses her cheek. "I will always be your mother. Even if you become fully human and I stay a vampire. Nothing will change." The confidence in her mother's eyes gives her a sense of relief. She knows she can trust in her words, and she will desperately hold on to her promise. Nothing will change, except everything. But they will find a way to make it work.

Nietta nods and then lifts a hand to reciprocate the warm gesture, by placing her hand on top of her mother's. "Thank you, Mom…" her voice cracks as she feels a rush of emotions washes over her, "for everything."

Hunter creeps into the room, after having given them a

long moment of space. Nietta and her mother break apart and turn to look at him. He smiles gently which causes a smile to stretch across Nietta's own lips. "Sorry don't mean to interrupt," he says, sheepishly scratching the back of his head. Nietta can't help but admire how adorable he looks with his cheeks blown up the way he does when he's feeling awkward.

"Not at all," her mother replies as she turns to face forward. "We were actually just starting to discuss what the shaman had told you. So, it's better that you be involved." Hunter nods in understanding as he makes for the empty armchair. He settles in as the atmosphere turns serious.

"So, what are our options?" he asks. Nietta feels a sense of amusement bubble in her chest at the way he positions himself, the tone he takes, as if they are in a business meeting.

She clears her throat and decides that she too needs to take this seriously. This could end up meaning life or death. The sire vampire has been a vampire for a lot longer than she has, how long she doesn't know, but he most definitely retains more strength and control than she does. Killing him will be so much more difficult than it is to kill a human. If they don't plan this strategically, then it could end with her being the one to meet her demise.

"He lives in the mountains of Massachusetts," her mother begins her explanation as Nietta and Hunter both lean in to give her their full attention. "From what I gather he was turned at the age of thirty-three and has been a vampire for about eighty years now."

Nietta's breath catches in her throat at the numbers spilling out of her mother's mouth. "That's a long time," she mutters in shock as she realizes that he is now over 100 years old. A heavy weight settles on her shoulders as she tries her best to digest the new information.

"Yes," her mother replies in a firm tone, "it won't be an easy task to kill him. But you will have to set out early in the day and make sure you get there a good amount of time before the sun sets. Both of you will be weakened by daylight, but most likely he will gain more strength than you during nighttime. Perhaps you will even be able to withstand the sun, just a little better thanks to your human side."

It is all speculation and interpretation. Nietta is fully aware of this, but even then, it makes her feel just a slightly bit more hopeful. If her mother is right, then she could potentially find a way to catch him off guard.

"I'll go with you," Hunter perks up, "I'll be there to support you. Maybe we could at least outnumber him."

Nietta's mother shakes her head."Vampires may be stronger at nighttime, but they aren't completely useless during daytime. He'd still be able to overpower you with a mere flick of his wrist." Her eyes grow sad. "I wish more than anything that I could come with you, as well, but as he is the vampire who turned me, I am sired to him which means I can't use my powers against him." Her mother hesitates as her gaze turns toward the ground. "Worst case is that he could even potentially use his sire powers to turn me against you."

Nietta nods as the information sinks in. She has always fought her own battles and this time is no different. She must go at it alone and she too feels it is the right choice. But the realization of having to fight the sire vampire without help does weigh heavy on her.

"I'll go with," Hunter says again, this time in a more decisive tone. "I understand the risks and I don't want to get in the way. But at least let me drive you there." His eyes beg her to agree and she can feel her heart bloom at his stubbornness.

"Okay," she whispers as her head bobs up and down, "you can come. But only if you stay in the car."

"Okay," he replies as he sits back in his chair. A proud smile plants itself on his face as Nietta gives in. *He sure does love to win,* Nietta thinks in amusement as she rolls her eyes in amusement.

"We've got to formulate a strong plan then," her mother pipes up as her eyes flicker between the two. This is no time for play. This is "do or die."

CHAPTER 17
DO OR DIE

They set out before dawn in Hunter's car as they head out to Massachusetts to find the sire vampire. Her mother claimed to keep tabs on him—after he moved out of Providence—utilizing the connections she had made through her journey into the vampire world. She told Nietta that being thrown into this whole new life had been scary and lonely, but she had been so thankful to stumble upon such helpful and understanding vampires that had helped teach her how to fully embrace her vampire side.

Although Nietta still felt a slight resentment toward her mother for not choosing her, she could understand at least a little bit now why her mother was so intent on living amongst the vampires. After having been abandoned and mistreated by so many humans, it must have meant everything to her to meet the vampires that took her under their wings without hesitation.

At first, the drive is silent as they both try their best to wake up. They had spent a lot of time the day before going through all the possibilities of what could potentially happen.

They had even gone into the night but had to let it go after they realized that they needed sleep to make sure they had energy for the early drive. On top of that, Nietta needed the energy for the ensuing fight.

She sits in silence as she stares out the window, the radio plays on low volume in the background as Hunter focuses on driving. To pass the time, she finds herself aimlessly counting how many trees they pass, which quickly becomes an impossible task. Although she wants nothing more than to distract herself from her impending doom, her mind is unable to come up with anything other than possible scenarios of fighting the sire vampire. A majority of them end with her death.

Hunter clears his throat which pulls her attention to him. "What are you thinking about?" he asks as he quickly throws her a glance before returning his focus to the road. He looks just as nervous as she feels, if not more. Somehow seeing his state of agitation makes her feel validated. At least she isn't going through this completely alone.

"I keep thinking about ways in which this fight might end," she admits as she turns her gaze toward her hands lying in her lap. She fidgets with her cuticles as she tries not to start picking at them. She used to bite her nails all the time when she was younger, but she was able to drop that habit years ago. For some reason, the urge has returned.

"And what way do you think it will end?" he asks, his tone void of any emotion. She knows that he is trying his best to be neutral so as to not influence her emotions with his.

"To be honest, I'm not sure if I have found enough confidence yet," she admits as she sinks further down into her seat. "I keep imagining different ways in which he kills me than ways in which I defeat him."

Hunter reaches out his hand and places it on top of hers, "We have more to lose, and if we follow the plan that the shaman set out for us, then we'll win. Together." His grip around her hand tightens as she feels the tug toward him tighten.

He's right. It's not about whether she will be able to defeat him, it is more so that she has to. They spent so long coming up with the best plan of action and all of her loved ones are counting on her.

She must think of them. She must win for them. She must win for herself.

CHAPTER 18
SILVER LININGS

As Nietta stands at the door of the sire vampire's house, she thinks about how she wished they'd had more time to revisit their plan. Had they truly done enough to prepare. Although they did consult the shaman on the exact steps of the ritual before taking off, the realization that it will be more difficult to actually execute dawns on her as she stares up at the large brick mansion. She decides the best option is to approach him head-on. She rings the doorbell and waits. Time feels like it's moving in slow motion as she stares at her white sneakers. She can feel the air come to a standstill as her heart rate slows down. She had insisted on Hunter waiting for her in the car, and although she still thinks it is the right choice to keep him —a human—out of this fight, part of her wishes he could stand beside her for support.

The door finally swings open and there stands a man around 5'11 with eyes as dark as night, hair golden as the sun, and a thin beard tracing the sharp outline of his jaw. He looks confused at his surprise guest as he stares at her with blank curiosity. She feels a chill run down her spine as she tries to find anything human about him. His eyes like deep, black pits stare back at her void of any deeper emotions. He looks at her as if she were a mere stain on his shoe.

"How can I help you?" he asks as he looks her up and down. He's got a strong build, and toned muscles that stand out even in his loose-fitted clothes. Despite not being that much taller than Nietta, it feels as if he is towering over her. Already overpowering her.

"I'm Nietta," she introduces herself slowly trying to play it cool, pretending that she is there for a simple conversation. "I would like to speak to you about an incident from the past."

His eyebrows raise and Nietta thinks she can almost read a flash of amusement on his face. But it is gone before she can even register whether it was real or just a figment of her imagination. "Can't say I am very keen on speaking about the past," he replies in a cold tone. Then he smiles, an eerie smile that throws Nietta off kilter. He steps aside and motions for her to enter. "Why don't you come in and I can see if I can help you."

She steps over the threshold as she does everything in her power to keep from trembling. Even her vampire seems to taunt her from within at how scared she is. *Coward,* she hears her vampire whisper as she hisses back mentally. The sire vampire leads her into his living room and offers her a seat on his couch, which she hesitantly accepts. As she sits down, the handle of the silver knife in her pocket digs into her leg as it is pushed up against her by the tightening of her trouser's fabric.

"Can I get you anything to drink, Miss..." He tilts his head as he waits for her to introduce herself.

"Nietta," she says as she tries to swallow the lump forming in her throat. She can't let him notice how abnormally nervous she is. Fortunately, he doesn't know what she is usually like so perhaps he just assumes she is a generally nervous person.

"Right," he says, still giving off no signs of emotion other than indifference. "It seems as though you don't exactly know who I am?" He places a hand on his chest in a grandiose manner as if appalled that she doesn't know him. As if he were a celebrity that everyone should know.

She shakes her head as she realizes that her mother never actually told her what his name is. "I know of you, but I don't know your name," she whispers, wondering if he'd find it odd that she came all this way for someone she doesn't even know the name of.

"Charles Silva, but all my friends call me Charlie." His lips stretch into a robotic smile once again. She can't help but feel her blood run cold. How could her mother ever have trusted this man? "So, drink?"

She decides that it would be a good chance to pull herself together, "Yes, some tea would be nice thank you." He nods and then heads off into what she can only imagine is the direction of his kitchen. The size of his manor causes Nietta to become even more nervous. There are so many places for him to hide and in case she would be the one trying to hide, where would she even do that? In such an unfamiliar environment any place would seem like a hiding place to her.

As she hears him start to prepare the tea in the kitchen, she decides to get up and at least get a good feel for the living room and the foyer. Right above the living room is a mezzanine that reveals at least two doors on the top floor, which she can only guess what they lead to. The living room consists of a large seating area with an L-shaped couch, a few chairs, a coffee table with a glass surface, and a large flat screen hanging above a brick fireplace. To the left of the foyer is a dining room which merely consists of a large mahogany dining table and ten chairs. Just as she is about to venture into the hallway behind the living room, Charlie reappears with her tea.

"Where are you heading off to?" he asks skeptically as he places her mug down on the coffee table in front of the spot, she had just been sitting in.

"Sorry," she mutters as she desperately racks her brain for an excuse that doesn't sound suspicious. "I was just admiring your house."

For a moment he merely stares at her, possibly trying to gauge whether she is telling the truth or not. He nods slowly and then answers, "Yes, it has been in the family for ages. I moved here about fourteen years ago after my uncle decided that Massachusetts was no longer for him. In fact, America altogether was no longer for him."

As he explains the backstory of how he had managed to inherit the manor from his uncle, Nietta finds her mind racing for ideas. When does she attack? How does she attack? But her train of thought cuts off as he stops trailing around the living room and turns to her. "But this is not what you came for," he says with finality, "I would like to know the true purpose of your visit to Nietta." He settles down in one of the chairs furthest from where she is sitting on the couch. He crosses his legs and spreads his arms as if to assert authority.

She clears her throat as she prepares for a possible attack. "In 1998, you turned a pregnant woman into a vampire." His lips twist into a sneer as he takes in what she is saying. "That woman was my mother."

"So, what? You're here for vengeance?" he asks as he continues to glare at her with hostility. She notices that his posture has changed as he now leans forward in a defensive manner.

She slowly gets up as he watches her carefully. "I came for answers." It isn't completely false, but it isn't the entire truth either. First, she'll have her inquisition and then she'll have her revenge.

"Answers?" he repeats slowly as she moves around the opposite side of the coffee table. He scoffs ."As if I owe anyone answers."

She looks at him head-on as she begins her questioning, "Why did you turn her?"

He rolls his eyes. "Look, child, some people are just unfortunate. Wrong place, wrong time." He twists his wrist in the air as he pushes out his bottom lip, already dismissing the conversation. "It's kind of like how human couples want babies. I wanted to spread my seed, so to say." He looks almost amused with his answer as if he had all the right to ruin another person's life for his own selfish needs.

She trails her hand up the side of her trousers as she prepares to attack. He meets her gaze one more time as she continues in her path around the coffee table toward him. She is no longer shaking.

"Your mother was too weak to be anything useful, so I abandoned her. I guess I made the right choice seeing as her daughter turned out to be just as stupid—" As soon as he insults her, Nietta is on top of him with the knife in her hands. She barely nicks the side of his throat as he grabs her by the neck and has her pinned up against the wall.

"You didn't think you'd get me that easily, did you?" He spits, centimeters away from her face. She tries to struggle as she realizes that he is much stronger than her. "Time to say goodnight," he rips her off the wall and throws her against the fireplace. Her back arches backward as she screams out in pain. Tumbling to the ground, he doesn't give her a chance to recuperate before he is on top of her again.

Her vampire wakes up just as he bares his fangs at her. *Not today,* her vampire laughs inside her mind as she cuts his arm. He is caught off guard by her sudden increase in strength. Nietta was right to subdue her vampire for just long enough to catch him off guard.

"Fucking bitch," he screams as he grabs his arm, now drenched in blood. She takes the opportunity of his confusion to roll out from underneath him. Just as she gets up to run, he grabs her by the hair and jerks her back into the fireplace. Once again she screams in pain as the bricks fall around her. He doesn't stop there as he picks her up and throws her onto the coffee table. The glass breaks beneath her weight as the shards rip her skin apart.

She tries to scramble out of the table but everywhere she puts her hand a new fragment rips through her skin. He looms over her as she stares up at him in sheer fear, there is no way she can win this. There is no way.

"As I said, worthless—" Before he can even finish his sentence a gunshot goes off as his body jerks to the left. Surprised, he stares down at the bullet wound in his left breast. He looks up to see Hunter standing in the doorway, gun in hand. "Guns don't kill vampires." He laughs, but it causes him to wince as blood continues to pour out of the wound.

"No, but silver bullets laced with the blood of a sired vampire do slow you down," Hunter replies as he lowers the gun. His face is fearful, afraid that the shaman was wrong. But, Nietta doesn't waste time as she shoots out of the table and wraps herself around the back of Charlie.

She slits his throat with her silver knife. They watch him sink to the ground. She bends down, rolls him over, and looks him dead in the eyes, "This one's for my mother." She rips his head clean off as her vampire strength runs rampant with the incomplete mating bond driving her insane. Hunter had even cut into his skin after she left to cause her cravings to heighten all her senses the moment he arrived at the scene. She feels unstoppable as she shoves the knife deep into Charlie's chest and cuts out his heart.

As soon as she has his heart inside her hands she finally lets go and collapses backward onto the ground. Although successful, she is bleeding profusely and the world before her swims.

The last thing she hears is Hunter calling out to her as he rushes to her side.

CHAPTER 19
'TIL DEATH...

The birds chirp a lovely tune in the distance as Nietta—aged sixteen—ventures through the empty fields, picking up leaves and flowers as she loses herself in a train of thoughts. She hums a soft tune to herself as the tall grass tickles the skin of her legs just below her jean shorts. She bends down to rip up a yellow star grass and hears a branch crack in the distance. A deer bounds out of the forest and into the field. It freezes when it notices her presence.

She stands up straight as she and the deer stare at each other. Its two bead-like eyes watch her with cautious fear as she feels a strange ache blooming in her stomach. Mesmerized by how close to the animal she is for the first time in her life, she takes in its golden fur that looks like it has been painted on in long, flowy strokes, its white polka dots that look like snowflakes on an abstract painting, and its big ears like a cartoon character. Its sweet appearance draws Nietta in as she wonders if she'd be able to pet it.

With each slow step toward the creature, she feels the aching in her stomach grows. Something sharp touches her lips from inside her mouth. Confused, she tilts her head downwards to touch her teeth that have grown into fangs. As she looks down, however, she notices a large red patch on the leg of the deer. Blood.

Her mother had warned her many times that one day her fangs would grow in and that day would be the day she would be overcome by a desire to kill so strong that she would lose all sense of herself and the world around her. Nietta could now finally understand what her mother was trying to say as one second, she was sharing a beautiful moment with a deer and the next the world has gone black.

When she comes to the deer is laying in her arms, lifeless, with its blood dribbling down her chin. Once she realizes what she has done tears start to roll down her cheeks as she shrieks out in fear. Fear for the reality of who she is becoming.

The breeze caresses Nietta's cheek softly as Hunter pulls her out of the car. He lifts her into his arms as he rushes into the shaman's shop.

"She's lost a lot of blood." His voice sounds desperate, afraid as the girl they met last time they came rushes to get the shaman. She reappears with her great-grandfather hanging onto her arm. The shaman urges them into the back of the store, into their flat.

"Lay her down here," he says as Hunter places her gently on their wooden floors. It's cold on the ground. Colder than it was in Hunter's arms. She feels that she is barely hanging onto life at this point and wonders if it would just be better to go in his arms. What if they try to save her and she ends up dying anyway?

"Hunter..." she mumbles as she tries weakly to reach out to him, but she can barely even move her fingers at this point.

"Shhh..." He kneels on the ground next to her and tries to comfort her by caressing her hair. "You're OK. We're going to find a way to help you." He keeps stroking her hair as the shaman scrambles to gather all of his tools in the background.

"Just focus on me. Keep fighting." His words of encouragement light a fire within the depths of Nietta.

Her vampire grumbles awake. She's losing control and she can feel her cravings kicking in as she yearns for blood.

"She needs to feed," the shaman says as he scrambles over to Hunter's side. "I can commence the ritual, but it would be too risky in her current state."

Nietta loses herself in Hunter's eyes as she tries to keep awake. Somewhere in the distance, she can hear a soft humming calling out to her. Almost as if trying to soothe her to eternal sleep. She thinks she can make out the tune to Golden Hour and for a second she loses focus. Then she feels the warmth of Hunter's touch on her face, and she is back again.

"Stay with me," he says desperately, "I will give you my blood." The shaman hands him a silver knife which causes Nietta's heart to lurch into her throat. In this state, she doesn't know how she will be able to restrain herself from draining him completely.

"No," she mutters, but she has no strength left to resist as he cuts into the flesh on his forearm and hovers it over her lips. "No," she mutters again but the moment a drop of his blood hits her lips her vampire flies out and latches onto his arm. He yelps in surprise as her fangs rip into him. She starts sucking and she can't stop.

The blood causes her to lose her thoughts completely as she replenishes her thirst. She can feel all her strength return as his blood courses through her system. Her vampire is so addicted to the rush of blood that she finds it hard to stop herself.

As she succumbs to the blood, she finds her mind wandering to all their memories. The first day they met, the day that he proposed, the day he showed up at her workplace. All of the emotions of those memories course through her brain as she meets Hunter's loving gaze. She feels a sense of completeness washes over her as she finally finds the strength to let go.

After taking a moment to breathe, she sits up and faces him. He looks weak from all the blood she took, but she was thankfully able to stop just in time.

His hand reaches out to her as he smiles in relief. "I love you," he mutters as he collapses into her arms. She can feel him breathing against her chest and knows he's OK. She didn't take enough for him to pass out, but he must be feeling pretty dizzy.

"I love you too," she replies as she wraps her arms around him. In the warmth of his embrace, she feels the tug toward him dissipate as she realizes that the mating bond has been completed. They are now, and forever will be, one.

CHAPTER 20
AND EVER AFTER

While Nietta and Hunter rest to regain their strength, the shaman sets about to complete the preparations for the ritual. He draws symbols that Nietta can't recognize, on the floor and all over the table. He sets the sire vampire's heart inside a chalice and lights candles.

"It's time," he finally says after a couple of hours. He turns to Nietta and gives her a strong nod. She returns the gesture and gets up to take her place within the setup. Hunter's hand finds hers as she passes him. She stops to look at him curiously.

"If it doesn't work, just know we will find a way regardless." He tries to comfort her, but she doesn't want to even consider the fact that the ritual could end up as a failure. They've worked so hard and put in so much effort to get to this point. There is just no way that it won't work. She offers him a half-hearted smile, however, and then continues toward the shaman.

"Sit here," he says as he pulls out one of the chairs at the table.

She sits down gently and then closes her eyes, uncertain of what's to come.

"I have never performed this ritual before," the shaman says in warning as he clears his throat. "Therefore, I can neither guarantee that it will work nor can I tell you what to expect." He moves a few things around and then takes a few steps back, finally satisfied with his setup. "It may be extremely painful and slow, or it may be quick and uneventful." He takes a huge breath and then finally asks, "Are you ready?"

Nietta gazes at the articles placed out before her in a sporadic manner. She reminisces about how life as a vampire has been and ponders how life will be as a human. For so long, she has been so dead set on becoming human that she never truly weighed out the two options. She never actually thought she would have another option. But now that she is here, about to fulfill her wish, there are no doubts left in her mind. "I am ready."

"Let's begin."

For a good few minutes, nothing happens as the shaman sits down on the floor next to her and chants. She doesn't recognize the language and therefore has no idea what he is saying. She feels merely confused as she waits patiently for the ritual to end or for something to change.

Heat pulses through Nietta's body as the shaman gets up to prance around the table. He continues to chant as the heat spreading through Nietta's body intensifies. The wooden chair she sits in feels as if it's digging into her skin the more and more her senses heighten. She feels her vampire trying to fight back against the ritual, trying to survive. Stars fly behind her eyes as the rage of her vampire increases. She can feel the vampire within screaming to be left alone, to continue living.

An invisible, sharp pain stabs her in the gut and knocks the breath out of her lungs. She opens her mouth to scream but nothing comes out. Lurched over the table, she uses all the strength she has left to stay in place. It's almost as if her vampire is trying to knock her out of her chair.

The memory of the first time that she fed flashes before her eyes. The deer hung loosely in her arms. She remembers all the times she used her abilities to escape and run away. She remembers all of the innocent people she killed due to her uncontrollable cravings.

This is it, she thinks with a resolution, *this is where we say goodbye.* Another sharp pain courses through her as she feels like a part of her is being ripped. She chokes on her own saliva as she is flung backward in her chair. With her neck bent backward, she stares at the empty white ceiling as her vampire disappears. One last shock courses through her body before everything comes to a standstill. The shaman stops chanting and moving around. Her mind is awfully silent for once. She feels free.

"It is done," the shaman says finally and then stands in front of Nietta who is bent over, huffing and puffing. "How do you feel?" The shaman asks curiously waits for Nietta to catch her breath.

For a moment she tries to take awareness of her body, mentally scanning every crevice of her being. "Different," she finally mutters, unsure of exactly how to describe this new sensation. The world around her seems so muted. The sounds have grown quiet, she can't pick out the details of things that are far away and the smells don't overwhelm her with nausea. Best of all, the idea of blood revolts her rather than exciting her. "I feel human." She chuckles. She gets up and runs over to Hunter, she jumps straight into his arms. He feels so much stronger than her now. "I'm human." She smiles down at him. He smiles back at her and wraps her into a tight hug. "Oh," she exclaims at the sudden squeeze. She can no longer take as much force as she used to. She coughs and Hunter quickly lets go. "Sorry, I'm not as strong as I used to be."

"Welcome to the human world," he replies in amusement, and they share a soft laugh.

The shaman approaches them as they break apart and Nietta looks over expecting a look of relief. Instead, he wears a look of uncertainty. "What's wrong?" she asks, wondering if they were celebrating prematurely.

"Well," he starts as he searches for the right way to go about his explanation, "I was unable to remove the vampire venom—" Nietta's heart sinks. Is it all just in her head? Was she just pretending to feel human because she wanted it so badly? "I was however able to make it dormant."

"What does that mean?" Nietta asks.

The shaman smiles in reassurance as he continues, "It means that the vampire venom will continue to exist within you, but it has been rendered inactive. In other words, it won't affect you in any way, unless you decide to turn into a vampire. That's the only time it could potentially cause you issues."

"What kind of issues?"

"Well, for one it could mean total disaster for not only yourself but also the rest of the world. You'd have double as much vampire venom in you than any other vampire. You could potentially lose complete control of yourself, altogether."

Nietta and Hunter share a look before she quickly reassures Hunter, the shaman, and herself, "I'm never going to turn into a vampire, ever again." She wonders if there would ever be a circumstance in which she could turn back into a vampire. But then again why go through everything she has to become human, just to throw it all down the drain?

Hunter smiles as he caresses her cheek. "Of course not."

The shaman nods in understanding. "Well, in that case, I do believe there is nothing for you to worry about. The ritual has been completed and my work here is done."

They all shake hands as Hunter and Nietta thank the

shaman profusely for everything he has done for them before heading back to Nietta's place. As soon as they get back, Nietta finds her mother there waiting for them. They share a long, warm embrace as her mother cries explaining how worried she had been. For a few minutes, they sit down and fill her in on everything that had happened before heading off to bed. It's been a long few days and there is nothing more that Nietta wants at this point than the comfort of her own bed.

———

Life has never been as ordained and beautiful in its simplicity as it has since Nietta became human. After everything with fighting off the cravings, the mating bond, the sire vampire, and finally the ritual that made Nietta human, it was surprisingly comforting to return to their normal jobs. Only a month after returning to normal did Hunter move in with Nietta.

Despite having led a mostly human life up until this point, Nietta found that there was still some adjusting to do. It was nice to have Hunter so close to help her readjust to life without her vampire abilities. They did everything that they used to do when they were together in a relationship the first time, but this time it was a lot easier.

Nietta found that she fell even deeper for Hunter with the obstacle of her fears around being a dhampir completely gone. They went on dates, planned their lives together, and even talked about kids in the future. Children. Something Nietta never thought she would be open to. Finally, she wouldn't have to worry about bringing another dhampir into this world.

Five months after becoming human, Hunter had decided they would take a trip back to their hometown in Providence. He brought her up to the bridge where he proposed to her for the first time. As he got down on one knee, Nietta was herself alight with joy. This time around, she was finally able to accept his proposal. She was finally able to promise him a future where they live out the rest of their lives together.

For a long time, Nietta had been running, running, and running from the monster that lay within her. She had been running from her past mistakes and running from the things she truly desired. In her mind, she would never be worthy of happiness because of the monster within. But once she was finally able to face that monster and defeat it, she was able to stop running away and start running toward the future. A future where she no longer has to kill to survive. A future where she can finally embrace the person she is. A future where she can finally stand beside Hunter as an equal.

A future of hope.

Sign Up To Receive My Newletter For All The Latest Updates and Specials!

RENEEJOINERAUTHOR.COM/NEWSLETTER

SUPPORT ME BY LEAVING A REVIEW!

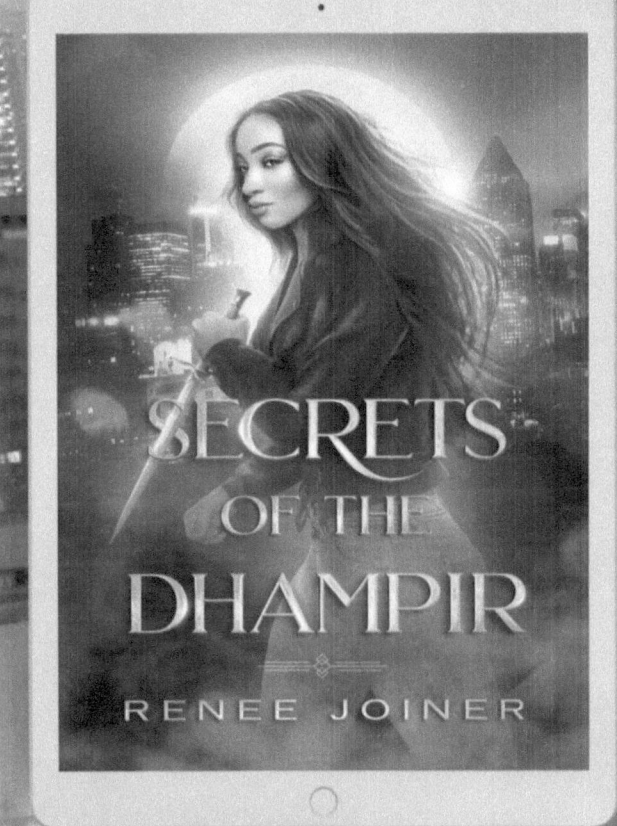

reneejoinerauthor.com/Dhampir_book

ABOUT THE AUTHOR

Renee Joiner has been in love with the supernatural for longer than she can remember, so it is no surprise that she is an author of paranormal urban fantasy. Although she discovered her passion for writing when she was only twelve years old, she didn't make her writing debut until many years into the future. Adventurous and fun-loving, she enjoys traveling to new places, exploring new sights and meeting new people. Thus, she delights in creating fantastical worlds that are sure to give her readers an escape from the real world while simultaneously providing thrilling entertainment.

Besides her special knack for writing, you'll also find a passion for metaphysics spirituality which she has been nurturing for over four decades. Renee hails from New York and currently resides with her husband in their empty nest—unless you count their three adorable fur babies—in Florida. She enjoys adding to her sea of knowledge and thus spends her free time learning new things.

To find out more about Renee Joiner, feel free to visit her **official website**.

facebook.com / reneejoinerauthor

twitter.com / iamreneejoiner

instagram.com / reneejoinerauthor

amazon.com / author / reneejoiner